In Praise of Navigation

In Praise of Navigation

Twentieth Century Stories from the Dutch

Edited by PC Evans & Paul Vincent

seren

Seren is the book imprint of
Poetry Wales Press Ltd
57 Nolton Street, Bridgend, Wales CF31 3AE
www.seren-books.com

ISBN 978-1-85411-416-7

This publication was made possible thanks to the financial support of
the Foundation for the Production and Translation of Dutch Literature.

Cover image: 'Chamber' 2006, by Emrys Williams; oil and wax on canvas, 36ins x 36ins.

The publisher works with the financial assistance of the
Welsh Books Council.

Printed in Plantin by Creative Print and Design, Wales

Contents

Introduction I

In his first lecture every history undergraduate is confronted by EH Carr's treatise 'What is History'. A fine laxative for the mind, but any successful student's essay will conclude that all history is merely subjective interpretation founded on disputable facts that we then manipulate to support our arguments.

This book is subtitled 'Twentieth Century Short Stories from the Dutch'. In order to nail down the fluttering butterfly of the *ding an sich*, one might be inclined to consider three questions: what is a short story, when, or what, was the twentieth century (at least in the Netherlands), and what is particularly different, but also common, about these Dutch writers that demands an anthology devoted especially to them? Kant's *ding*, of course, was never to be exposed. Here, nevertheless are some general observations on the Dutch environment that may help to contextualise the very divergent writers included in this collection.

The Dutch poet Martinus Nijhoff once wrote 'On this spot there used to be a poem. I didn't like the look of it.' The opening story of this collection was originally 'Little Poet' by Nescio (unfortunately now AWOL due to permission issues). The history of the modern Dutch short story begins with Nescio. 'Little Poet' is significantly dated 1917 and bears the inscription 'In the Year of the War, *Bellum transit, amor manet* (War passes, love remains)'. Could Robert Graves or Wilfred Owen have written this in a stinking trench in 1917? The story has the tone of an erudite pavement-café writer somewhat removed from the backdrop of the European apocalypse. Somewhat removed, somewhere on the sidelines holding the coat of history. This has often been the state in which Holland has bobbed along over the last couple of centuries (something we were graphi-cally reminded of with the recent performance of Dutch soldiers at Srebrenica, the Dutch government riding on the coattails of the international community, the official pseudonym for the American and British war machine).

Of the pre-war period Yeats has stated that the writers he knew were still living in a Tristan and Isolde dream world, rudely shattered by The Great War and the advent of Messrs Pound, Eliot and Joyce. It is axiomatic that modern literature in English finally stormed the Georgian barricades with the First World War. But in Holland where was this catalyst to letters? The rude jolt that catapulted English liter-ature into facing the concerns of the modern world in a contemporary idiom was considerably less dramatic in the Dutch experience, where the major concerns were a downturn in trade and the annoyance of a scarcity of potatoes. One is mindful of Orson Welles' comment about Switzerland: after five hundred years of neutrality their only contribu-tion to world culture was the cuckoo clock.

'Little Poet' (and of course 'Sponger') by Nescio, are two of the defining, and aesthetically satisfying, short stories of the period, but the story that was originally meant to be included here still possesses something of the quality of Henry James, it is an intelli-gent and wry depiction of the manners and *mores* of Dutch society at the turn of the twentieth century, an ossified world of a sterile bourgeoisie, even removed from the socialist agitation of this period. Modernism, despite the Belgian Paul van Ostaijen's 'Music Hall' of 1916, did not occur as a seismic paradigm shift as else-where in Europe in 1917 or 1918, or as one big bang as in Britain in 1922. Some would argue that modern, or Modernist, literature only reached its zenith with the publication of Martinus Nijhoff's *New Poems* in 1934. Others have claimed that the major revolution in literature was only brought about by the Second World War and the advent of the new generation of experimentalist writers in the 1950s, though these writers might more accurately be equated with the American Beats. Thus far, some observations on the tone and historical context, but we have yet to engage the specific 15,500 words that constitute what we designated as the short story 'Little Poet'. Designated because we weren't adequately able to translate the title, the very first word, which can lead to some serious miscomprehensions as biblical scholars have also discovered.

In Dutch the word for poet is '*dichter*'. The sixteen million inhabitants of the Netherlands are proud to live on a fertile dollop of mud and sand no bigger than a postage stamp, and with about as much room to move as the shipwreck survivors on Gericault's 'Raft of the Medusa', and with the very real possibility that the next wave might wash them all off. In order to humanise their habitat, the human battery chickens have invented the diminutive suffix 'je' or 'tje', which they add to their nouns to make everything petite, cute and cosy. By adding 'tje' to *dichter*, the modified noun both reduces and satirises the particular poet in this story, though in a sweet way. If it had concerned a writer (*schrijver*) the addition of the 'tje' might have required the word to be translated as 'scribbler'. But there is no ready common English word to render the subtle demotion of this particular poet to a poetaster. The diminution of the poet is also revealing of the attitude of Dutch society, which in its post-religious sobriety still punishes any affectation. At the time of the composition of this story it was still common to belittle the excesses and talents of Van Gogh, for example.

Clearly the Dutch, like all cultures, have undergone a social and semantic history that is entirely their own. Words and phrases have arisen from specific social and historical circumstances, and by repetition they have helped to form the mental structures of subsequent generations. Just last night a friend was here for dinner and told us of her recent gynaecological examination. Without any sense of etymological baggage she revealed how her doctor had informed her he was about to spread her 'lips of shame'. The Dutch pride themselves on being fiercely independent, individualistic and self-opinionated. It is thus sometimes amusing as an outsider to hear them expressing their identical individual opinions in the very same hackneyed phrases.

When once asked by a reviewer if he was proud of his latest Penguin novel, Harry Mulisch replied that of course he was pleased, but he also harboured a certain sense of detachment because he hadn't written a single word of it, his translator had. Harry Mulisch never wrote 'The Assault' or 'The Discovery of

Heaven', he wrote *'De aanslag'* and *'De ontdekking van de hemel'*.
The English translations are a recreation in another language,
almost another medium, by a different author. These Dutch
writers, like writers of any nationality, hew their work like sculptors
from the sounds, history and conventions of their own culture,
upon which they bring their originality to bear. Dutch is an entirely
different way of producing sound and a markedly different
medium of thought. One of the cheapest 'How to Speak Dutch'
books on the market begins with the word *'graag'* on page one,
which it inaccurately translates as 'please'. The 'gs' at the beginning
and end are two guttural 'chs' that sound like a couple of cats spitting venom at each other over a trapped rat in a filthy alley (a
hardness I've often heard replicated in the harsh accents of the
inhabitants of the Province of Holland, peopled for centuries by
hardnosed merchants and traders). The second consonant and
double vowel together sound like the Egyptian sun god or a visit to
the dentist. *Graag*. Clearly a folk that emits this noise to express
eagerness or pleasure has undergone its own unique trajectory of
experience. Even the word for sweetheart *'schat'* sounds like a
common assault with a blunt instrument. It reminds one of the Ted
Hughes poem 'Crow's First Lesson': ' "Say love," said God... Crow
gaped, and a bluefly, a tsetse, a mosquito/ Zoomed out and down/
To their sundry fleshpots', etc.

The Netherlands began its recorded historical life as a mosquito
infested swamp on the outskirts of the Roman Empire where the
legionaries could safely toast their crumpets on the friendly bank of
the Rhine. Charlemagne drew it more closely into the European
orbit, basing his capital just over the border at Aachen. The area,
nominally part of the Holy Roman Empire, was Christianised
somewhat later than the rest of Western Europe by the Welshman St
Boniface whom the natives boiled in a pot around 1550. Following
early success as a component of the Hanseatic League, the Golden
Age of the Netherlands truly began with the founding of
Amsterdam and its expansion within a few decades to become the
new Jerusalem of capitalism, international trade and relatively
liberal thought. The Netherlands inevitably struck out for inde-
pendence in the 1580s after growing bored with paying taxes to the

high-church, Johnny-foreigner Spanish Habsburgs. After a hundred-year explosion that saw the United Provinces of the Netherlands morph into the greatest sea power on earth, coveted and ultimately hamstrung by the avaricious English and French, the country settled into a slow decline then atrophy that saw it regress into something of a pleasant bourgeois backwater. Hemingway has written of Paris as 'a moveable feast', largely because of its impressive cast of artists and writers. Amsterdam, and the Netherlands in general, is a mild and decorative utopia, a compact universe of reasonableness on an often insane globe. Home to Erasmus and the Jew Spinoza, home away from home for Descartes and Locke, the Netherlands still likes to annoy its conservative neighbours with its enlightened policies on anything from euthanasia, to homosexuality, to drugs, and is religiously devoted to consultation and compromise over action, violent or otherwise.

The Second World War was the single most important event in the Dutch history of the twentieth century and is reflected as such in its literature. Hermans and Mulisch in particular have dealt extensively with this subject in their novels (Mulisch, of course, is the son of a Jewish mother and a Nazi father). Churchill once sketched how Britain would have looked if it had been invaded in 1940, with a puppet, pro-fascist government led by Oswald Mosley and active collaboration from the sizeable section of the population that was already psychologically predisposed to totalitarianism and anti-Semitism as well as the vast majority of floating voters who like to knuckle down and just get on with things – the sheep – and then of course you have the small percentage of brave souls who would have formed the military and trade union resistance. This is the situation in which Holland found itself after May 1940, an occupied country (raising the flag of neutrality had not helped this time), where morality, loyalty and simply negotiating everyday life were one great grey area.

The proportion of Jews deported from the Netherlands with the active collaboration of the police was higher than anywhere else in Europe; government documents declassified some years ago reveal that one in five Dutch citizens were actively spying for the Nazis. When British paratroopers were fighting in the streets of Arnhem a battalion of the Dutch SS *Landenstorm* was attached to the opposing

German SS *Hohenstaufen* Division. In his story 'Breaking the Silence',
Bernlef describes an unnamed Eastern European police state where
the majority of the population have been twisted into opportunistic,
malignant, self-righteous tattletales. But after the fall of the regime,
as Bernlef ironically points out, everyone actually appears to have
been a hero or had at least intended to be. This is the feel good myth
that took root in Holland after the war. The police and establishment
were riddled with collaborators and their position was rather expedi-
ently protected according to the 'better the Baathist you know than
the mullah you don't' principle. The anti-German strikes and the
privations of the Hunger Winter have perhaps fulfilled the role of
psychological absolution for the Dutch. In his story 'Paranoia'
Hermans deals with a purportedly Dutch SS soldier on the run, who
is hunted by the authorities for his crimes. It is indeed true that there
was a spate of reprisals and the head shaving of *moffenhoeren*, or
'kraut whores', in the wake of the liberation. But if you were to visit
the 'public' War Documentation Centre, you would discover that any
questions relating to Dutch NSB collaborators (in my case for a
documentary) would not be welcomed. Officially this is to protect
the offspring of the collaborators and criminals, but I am curious as
to what information is present relating to the policemen, bureaucrats
and future politicians who participated in the deportation of the Jews
and the murder of their own countrymen and yet were left unmo-
lested in their posts and careers.

Running along the west coast of the Netherlands there is a chain of
sand dunes that shelters the low-lying hinterland from the storms and
floods of the North Sea. Perhaps the most attractive section is the
Kennemmer Dunes, where the coarse grass and undergrowth knot the
sand into low hills topped by tall pines, through which a myriad of
paths meander, bordered by wild flowers, and populated by colonies
of rabbits and deer. Somewhere in the woods there are two pristine
lakes that on any fine day are dotted with children. It is here that the
Nazis brought Dutch resistance members to be executed. In a tiny
valley between two dunes there is a simple brick plaque marking one
of their mass graves; on a dune in the distance a large memorial cross
set against the sky. Mulisch's dichotomy is shared by many more
Dutch and European families than would care to admit it.

This anthology covers Dutch society and letters from the watershed of the nineteenth and twentieth centuries to the fall of the Iron Curtain. From the ethnically homogeneous but socially segregated world of Protestants, Catholics and Socialists, to the threshold of our ethnically diverse, religiously and socially divided modern Netherlands – where fifty per cent of the major cities are now populated by Turkish, Moroccan and other immigrants, where politicians, satirists and artists are threatened and sometimes murdered in the streets. A world that has not yet adequately been dealt with in serious Dutch literature or assimilated into the Dutch toleration model.

If anyone asked me to define a short story, I would probably hand them one of Chekhov's – perhaps 'The Trousseau' or 'The Troublesome Guest'. Something about eight or ten pages long, with strong characterisation, a compelling narrative and a well-worked-out plot finishing in an unexpected denouement. Several minutes of Googling yields various definitions that set the ideal length of a short story at anything from 6000 to 16,000 words, with the qualification that most of the world's best short stories have deviated from this pattern. This is certainly the case with work from the Netherlands. Dutch writers particularly seem to have a predilection for the short novella, as we can see in the work of Nescio, Bordewijk, Hermans and Rosenboom. In Holland, as in other countries, the short story appears to bear the status of a not wholly loved, adopted, child – a troublesome presence and a drain on the finances of publishers. Even such a great figure as Carver has been commiserated, post mortem, for not having published a novel, though perhaps the evidence of Hemingway's oeuvre suggests that it is best to settle for the genre that you are master of. Despite this, almost all of the writers in this anthology are also successful novelists or poets in their own right. Perhaps they can be seen as standard bearers of a form that has never set down the sort of deep roots in the national psyche that is has in the United States or Russia.

Stylistically this anthology was originally intended to move from the then shocking frankness of the late nineteenth century to the post-modern playfulness of Biesheuvel, if you can pigeon-hole such an original and idiosyncratic writer into any such classification. The

influence of the wider world is clearly evident in the work of these
writers and on society in general. Many of the authors included here
have also translated world figures ranging from Kafka to
Tranströmer. It is remarkable how many of the stories we have
anthologised are set in, or concerned with, the world beyond the
Netherlands, in the former Dutch Empire and further afield –
Debrot in the Caribbean colonies, Reve and Van Toorn in England,
Bernlef in Eastern Europe and Slauerhoff wherever the next tramp
steamer would take him. A culture that has sometimes been caught
mouthing at the window-pane of its own language is keen to
measure itself against the outside world. The work of these writers
can regularly be seen in indigenous magazines alongside translations of Borges or Mann; Dutch writers and poets frequently
appear on festival stages alongside their foreign counterparts and
one will often hear a Dutch artist described as perhaps the James
Joyce of Rotterdam or even the Dutch Woody Allen. In recent
decades Dutch authors have increasingly carved out their own position in international literature, particularly in Germany. Of the
authors included here, Bernlef has published novels with Faber, and
Claus and Mulisch have long enjoyed international success.
(Mulisch received his latest international award, the Nonino Prize,
from VS Naipaul only a week ago). In many ways the Netherlands
has sometimes resembled some exposed border region between
greater countries in cultural terms, tramped by foreign trends like
pillaging armies bent on some other destination. But what has
rooted is a Dutch literature that is entirely its own, *au fait* with world
literature, making use of it, but expressive of a consciousness, value
system and manner of seeing that are entirely its own.

PC Evans

* PC Evans is a poet and literary translator. He lives in Amsterdam and
South Wales. He has published poetry in Britain and Holland and translations of Dutch poetry, fiction and drama with Faber and Seren. He is
co-editor of the European literary magazine *The Amsterdam Review*.

Introduction II

In Praise of Navigation or Small is (as) Beautiful

Whole libraries have been written about the distinction between short stories and novellas on the one hand and fully-fledged novels on the other. For the purposes of this introduction, however, I propose to avoid controversial questions of demarcation and to speak simply of shorter fiction. To generalise, it is broadly true of Dutch-language writing, as it is of most European literatures I am familiar with, that the rise of shorter fiction dates from the beginning of the twentieth century. Up to then the field was dominated by bulky, often multi-volume novels, which Martin Amis once famously described as 'a fatal casualty of World War 1'.

Surveying the peaks of Dutch fiction in the nineteenth century, one sees virtually only novels, with such names as Conscience, Multatuli, Bosboom-Toussaint, Couperus and Streuvels dominant. The most striking exception is the small-scale Dickensian virtuosity of Nicolaas Beets in his *Camera Obscura* (1839). Around the turn of the twentieth century, however, there is a noticeable trend towards compression and concentration. After 1918 the successful and widely-translated novelist Louis Couperus (1863-1923) proves himself an adept writer of character and travel sketches, while his chilling supernatural story 'The Opera Glasses' ('*Het binocle*') is worthy of Edgar Allan Poe. At approximately the same time two original voices, one from the south and one from the north, emerge and make the small fictional canvas their own. In 1913 Willem Elsschot (ps. Alfons de Ridder, 1882-1960) published his *Villa des*

Roses, which was to be the first in a series of compact classics: set in a seedy Paris pension, Elsschot's début is an inspired reworking of the familiar boarding-house genre. The Amsterdammer Nescio (ps. JHF Grönloh, 1882-1961) paints unforgettable miniatures of bohemian life in the pre-1914 Netherlands.

Shorter fiction has thrived in the Low Countries ever since, with such accomplished novelists as Simon Vestdijk (1898-1971) and Hugo Claus (born 1929) proving themselves equally expert within a limited scope. The same is true of virtually all the writers represented in this collection, who have produced distinguished and in some cases classic longer works of fiction. A brief review will suffice to demonstrate the range and depth of talent contained in these pages.

J Slauerhoff (1898-1936) is remembered today principally as a 'doomed poet' in the grand romantic mould, but his fiction, with its occasional echoes of Conrad (Slauerhoff served as a ship's doctor), is unjustly neglected. In particular, the ambitious novel *Het verboden rijk* (*The Forbidden Kingdom*, 1932), which intertwines the lives of a nameless ship's wireless operator in the present, and that of the sixteenth-century Portuguese poet Luis de Camoens, who died in Macao, still awaits an English translation.

In his first work of fiction, the novella 'My Black Sister' (*Mijn zuster de negerin*, 1935), set on Curaçao, Cola Debrot (1902-1981) tackles the twin taboos of interracial love and incest as well as conveying an implicit critique of the colonial system. The book is regarded as the first landmark of Antillean literature in Dutch and is still unsurpassed.

Though not a gay rights activist, Anna Blaman (1905-1960) produced atmospheric fiction, including the novel *Op leven en Dood* (1954; tr. *A Matter of Life and Death*, 1974), that explored lesbian life and provided a pioneering validation of single-sex relationships.

Gerard Reve (ps. GK van het Reve, 1923-2006) captured the malaise of the younger generation in gloomy, austere post-war Amsterdam in *De avonden* (*The Evenings*, 1947; translation forthcoming) and in two later stylised books of open letters was the first Dutch writer openly to profess his homosexuality. Always a great stylist and humorist, Reve tended in later work towards mannerism and even self-parody, but the story included here belongs firmly to his 'vintage' period.

The prolific and versatile Harry Mulisch (born 1927), the youngest of the 'Great Trio' of post-war Dutch authors comprising WF Hermans (1921-1995), Reve and himself, has the highest international profile of any of the writers discussed. His novel *De aanslag* (1982; tr. *The Assault*, 1985) was adapted for the screen by Fons Rademakers and won an Oscar for the best foreign film of 1986. Mulisch is a gifted storyteller, and his most ambitious work of fiction to date, *De ontdekking van de hemel* (1992; tr. *The Discovery of Heaven*, 1996), chronicles the restoration to heaven of the Ark of the Covenant. It was also filmed, this time by Jeroen Krabbé with an English cast, but inexplicably has not yet been generally distributed outside the Low Countries.

An equally versatile figure, often described (like Mulisch) as 'a Nobel laureate in waiting' is the Fleming Hugo Claus who, besides fiction, writes poetry and drama and is also a painter. His magnum opus, *Het verdriet van België* (1983; tr. *The Sorrow of Belgium*, 1990), is a kaleidoscopic view of occupation and collaboration in Flanders seen through the eyes of a young, impressionable narrator.

Willem van Toorn (born 1935) is a poet, theatre critic and translator, besides the author of novels and stories that paint an often bleak but vivid picture of human relationships.

Bernlef (born 1937) won international acclaim with his moving study of Alzheimer's disease as experienced by a sufferer in the novel *Hersenschimmen* 1984 (tr. *Out of Mind*, 1988). He is a productive poet, novelist and translator (notably from the Scandinavian languages).

JMA Biesheuvel (born 1939) burst on the literary scene in the 1970s with his unique brand of linguistic virtuosity, eccentric humour, existential disorientation, obsession, madness and literary erudition.

Margriet de Moor (born 1940), has enjoyed considerable success abroad with such novels as *Eerst grijs dan wit dan blauw* (1991; tr. *First Grey, then White, then Blue*, 1994) and *De virtuoos* (1994; tr. *The Virtuoso*, 1996). However, De Moor, a former professional musician, first made her mark in fiction with volumes of stories and novellas in which the subtle modulations of her narrative style are already fully apparent.

Hopefully readers of this collection will agree that while the authors contained in it may on this occasion have chosen small craft in which to set sail, they, like their seafaring ancestors, are adventurous navigators, venturing imaginatively across wide expanses of ocean.

Paul Vincent

★ Paul Vincent studied at Cambridge and Amsterdam, and after teaching Dutch at the University of London for over twenty years became a full-time translator in 1989. Since then he has published a wide variety of translated poetry, non-fiction and fiction, including work by Achterberg, Bernlef, Boon, Claus, Couperus, Elsschot, Jellema, Martinus Arion, Mulisch, De Moor and Van den Brink.

Larrios

J Slauerhoff

Translated by Paul Vincent

(1930)

Was it a series of coincidences that led me to encounter you, unexpectedly, in places as far from each other as is possible on this earth? Why did I have to keep finding you again where I lost you more hopelessly each time? I can't believe in fate, since I could never share yours, scarcely even touch it, and I have not lived long enough to know whether I once changed its course.

Was it a series of coincidences? If not, what malevolent providence caused me to find you four times in the strangest circumstances and almost immediately lose you again?

It began long ago. Europe was not yet slowly dying, but the country I was travelling through was already dead. The extremities of a body whose strength is sapped can mummify at an early stage, while it lives on in apparent health. I travelled by train across the hot, hard plains, where the slopes are so gradual, where there are so few houses, where so few flocks graze and where so many boulders are strewn about and sharp rocks protrude like knuckles through dry skin. In one of the southern ports I had jumped ship, because the food on board was even more rotten than the minds of the villainous crew. I was hoping to find another in Bordeaux, if possible a better one. At first on foot, then hitching a ride on a lorry from the southern heat over the steep, icy ridge of the Sierra Nevada and descending back down to the hot plateau, I reached Granada in three days. I slept in a park and did not dare enter the princely Alhambra in my rags and tattered state of mind, but took the early morning train to Madrid, squatting for nearly two days in a third-class carriage where there were soldiers sleeping on the seats, in blankets on the dirty floor, already worn out by heaven knows what campaign against a *pronunciamiento* in the south. In Madrid I did not venture into the Plaza de Toros. I knew that the sight of blood would be unbearable. I walked frantically through the still deserted city and took the train further north and found myself in that strange delirious state after a long period of sleeplessness, in which one does not know if one is hungry or disgusted by food, exhausted or still capable of long marches. With an army like that one can win campaigns or suddenly lose everything in panic because a soldier throws down his rifle. I slept through every stop, every station and was finally woken when the train juddered to a halt. It was Burgos. In the distance the ponderous cathedral stood amid a flock of low grey houses, where the long train had stopped in front of a row of buildings built in the appalling tenement style one finds everywhere, even in dead Spain. I turned away and closed my eyes. The train was stationary for a long time and finally moved off with a jolt and my heart seemed to stand still, seized by some inexplicable despair at this departure. What could there be here in this town I had never visited and of which I knew nothing, save that it contained an old cathedral where Columbus was buried? I sprang to the window and saw nothing but the long balconies in front of the red brick houses divided by partitions from floor to gutter into a series of compartments. I was about to turn away, when you appeared on one of the verandas of the last block. That is when it began. You were leaning over the unpainted balustrade. At first you did not look up, though

I took you in at a glance from head to toe and from the surface of your skin to your very depths. You looked like so many Spanish women, a mantilla round your slim shoulders, though your stance betrayed an ability to move languorously and lithely, and of course a red flower in your excessively shiny hair. I couldn't see your eyes, but I guessed their colour and expression from the rest of your appearance. When you raised them just before we quickly passed you, a few metres from the train window, I was filled with dismay. They were full of a centuries-old suffering that has never succumbed to pain and subjugation, but rather has grown great in their presence and seems to be awaiting some unspoken impulse that will render it proud and irresistible, as if the long humiliation was the arbitrary product of a strange delight in testing yourself. You looked up at me and I forgot everything, even that I was being dragged past, and then I was awakened by the torment that is the lot of everyone suddenly faced by a huge decision, which if delayed by just a second can no longer be taken and if taken at once is eternally irrevocable. This is the true death agony, although in the midst of life, compared with which one's later demise is a painless drifting off, and I stood motionless and lost you, Larrios. I left you alone among enemies and perhaps your endurance was used up just at that moment and you could not help but collapse and fall prey to them. Thus I experienced your life compressed into a second and suffered it, carried along without moving. Then I flared up and might have jumped out, but at that moment you calmly laid your hand above your heavy eyebrows and saluted me with the other; there was no mistaking it. I was the only one leaning so far out of the departing train and I knew: you wanted to see me again and were imperiously summoning me. No perilous leap now; I would get off in Vittoria, walk back, if necessary hanging underneath a cart. But on the way back I was assailed by my old doubts and even despair: was she really different from many others in this country, who kneel pious and stupid and clean in the dark cathedrals with the same vacant devotion, whether they are sorely-tried wives or clapped-out whores. And if she carried a secret, did she know it herself, living in a paralysis from which no awakening was possible? Would she not laugh in embarrassment if someone came to her and said 'Look, my feet are raw, because I walked from Vittoria to Burgos for your sake.' 'Why did you walk?' 'Because I had no money and still wanted to see you again.' 'Why did you want to see me again if you had no money to pay for me?'

Why that gesture? Could it have been out of habit? To someone who was never coming back? But in the train I heard a conversation between businessmen who went back and forth from Bordeaux to Madrid by train every week. I didn't want to think anymore, but I couldn't sleep either. I stared vacantly out across the arid plains, when suddenly it became dark and threatened to rain and I saw another old cathedral, now standing alone and beneath the deep shadow which the sun broadens and narrows like the tides but never entirely erases, flowers stood shivering in the wind, red petals trembling, fluttering along the black damp stone. And then I closed my eyes. I got off in Vittoria, but was staggering before I left the platform, dizzy with hunger: I had no money, and my ticket to Bordeaux was my sole earthly possession. Larrios, do not forgive me my doubt or my suspicion, although they issued from the life I lead and not from myself; forgive me for going on, leaving you further and further behind; I would have been at death's door before I found you. In Bordeaux I was able to find a ship, recover, wait and search for you from the next port. I found a ship, but it was bound for Seattle; that was far away from you, but back then I thought death was even further away.

★

Then there was the second time. After ten months, constantly moving from ship to ship, I had reached Santander and could take the train to Burgos. I walked for days through the streets, sat in the cathedrals for hours, visited all the markets, waited till the factories emptied and heard many a sarcastic comment, but at night I roamed the sparsely lit streets; then, on one of those evenings, it became clear to me that I was not going to find you, since whoever found anything by looking? I could not stay any longer in Burgos, but nor could I leave Spain yet. I felt as if I were still close to you in this country. I headed south and one evening, after a long journey through the mountains, I reached

the dried-up river that joins the sea past the old Moorish town of
Málaga. I saw the town lying between two hills beneath the flaky
evening red: seedy white blocks with the black patches of abandoned
plots between. At the same moment it started to rain, the yellow
crumbling riverbed slowly filled with water that first turned the
bottom grey then started flowing through the many channels. The
mule trains that had first followed the soft river path now climbed
higher and straggled on down the stony path along the bank. The
beasts of burden carried the exhaustion of the long day in their
collapsed backs through the melancholy evening. I could not pass
them by walking faster. Whenever I sat down somewhere on the
verge, the muleteers went into a tavern and whenever I stood up they
had emptied their glasses and were moving on, just ahead of me. In
this way, bringing up the rear of this gloomy procession, I approached
the town. The rain had grown heavier. The river was now foaming
across its full width and carried dry bushes with it under the bridges.
I had eaten nothing but hard bread that day, I had not dared drink a
glass of wine – that makes it so hard to walk later. I was sweaty and
drenched by the rain; my clothes were sticking to my skin and I was
seized by the grey desolation known only by the wanderer approaching towns he has never visited, where the lights and the peace of
evening glow as if outside him. The suburbs began to expand. Low
black houses with deep-set broken windows; the mule train scattered
across a dark square and suddenly I was alone and missed the
company I had first cursed. I was not thinking of you at that point; I
cursed myself for traipsing around here instead of floating through
space on a ship. As I leant against a bridge, a figure came towards the
bank from a dark narrow street, skirts raised; a pale face glowed
beneath an umbrella – a lily emerging from a large enveloping black
goblet. She walked with light steps, as if relaxed after a hard day's
work. She came straight towards me and I saw that it was you, whom
I had almost stopped looking for, and with a strangely compassionate
gesture you held that umbrella over our heads and your shivering
body touched mine. I walked beside you without speaking, not
knowing what to do; I had waited too long, thought too much, and
finally with gentle pressure I tried to persuade you to drink a glass of
wine in a brightly lit tavern. But you laughed, grasped my sleeve,

wrung the water out and immediately pulled me after you. We went through countless alleys, climbed countless stairs. A small room, a shallow area of darkness behind two narrow windows; in it you lit a small lamp which immediately illuminated a brown statuette of the Madonna; then I saw your room: a bed, a table with sewing machine on it. On the wall two humdrum paintings, some earthenware dishes on a shelf – that was all. Even Japanese girls, who squat, sleep, do their hair, eat and give themselves to visitors on the same mattress, have more. A twig in a vase with a slender flower bending out of it, a screen with a flight of herons across it, an elegant fan.

You did not prepare yourself immediately like those eager to earn: the English women who say in their hoarse voices, 'have your short time', the Japanese saving hard for their dowry (though Spanish factories too pay far too little). You helped me out of my leaden clothes and wrapped me in a rough woollen robe. Had a monk left his habit together with his faith in your care? At any rate it was a warm robe. For a long time I shivered under the blankets while you finished your work and knelt before the brown statue, and then sang softly and monotonously, so that I lay awake and rested. It was late when you took off your robe and joined me. I did not demand much love of you: I soon fell asleep and, when the sun rose grey-red above the wall opposite, the place next to me was empty. What was I to do? I couldn't lie there all day. It was too hard for me with everything that I still had to say, that I had kept silent for years. I had only asked, 'Did you know in Burgos that I would return?' And you said, 'Yes, but not here'. I could stand it no longer, walked round a few streets and realised in a small noisy square that I was lost. What street had I come out of? With a shock of horror it flashed through me: found and immediately lost again, and I wandered through the tangle of narrow streets. I went back to the river and tried to find the way from there, climbed up and down steps, could not even remember if your room was on the fourth or the fifth floor: I knocked at many doors and was shooed away. In the afternoon I climbed up to the blistering Alcazador, hoping to discover from on high what I had not been able to find down below. I sat there on a chunk of rubble and my mind was a blank; I thought I saw a woman hanging out of the window with black hair and a red flower in it, and made as if to jump up, but a heavy weight on my shoulder forced me down. Gypsies were standing round me and a girl had set a full jug on my back; they were all laughing, but the girl saw my despair when I awoke, took the jug off my back and put it to my lips. In the evening I walked for hours up and down the brightly lit streets. Was I hoping to find you or find someone else with whom I could forget you? You know how despair confuses everything, hate and love.

★

I collapsed exhausted into the corner of a tavern and drank to numb myself; my head sank onto the table, I received a hard thump in the back and I sprang up to confront a heavily built man with a paunch, a red creased neck and watery eyes.

'What the hell d'you want?'

'A man: my quartermaster's run away.'

'Where are you going?'

'Everywhere; my ship's a good old tramp.'

Oh Larrios, if I couldn't find you in Málaga, why not everywhere? I took the offer, was given an advance of thirty pesetas, with which I bought some worn out equipment, and by evening I was lying in cramped quarters among the scum of the oceans.

The *Glenmore* wasn't a bad ship. Whereas on many vessels the hammock is the only place to rest and has to be hoisted out of the way by daybreak, here each of us had a cabin for a refuge: three high and three deep along the walls of the crew's quarters, but with a curtain you could close off an area and lie alone without being spied on. On the wall there was room for a few portraits or pictures: everyone seemed to like best what they had never seen. A Chinese man had decorated his wall with a Dutch windmill and a girl in traditional costume; the boatswain, a Norwegian, lay gazing at a geisha with a piled-up hairdo, with Mount Fuji behind him at the foot end. My wall remained empty. Whose portrait was I supposed to put up? I wanted only you before me, Larrios, and all I saw was your face, with all its features, and with my knife I drew lines when I could not get to sleep and slowly it grew into a likeness. The wood changed colour and one morning at first light I clearly saw your face: perhaps I was the only one, but I could see it. In full daylight it became indistinct again. Still I was afraid that someone else would see it, and when I found a face in an old *London News* that was vaguely similar, I covered the spot with it so that I could see you by moving the picture aside. The day came when because of a serious collision the *Glenmore* had to go into dock and we were all paid off. This was in Swansea; we were waiting for a ship in the seamen's hostel. At night I made my way across the wharf to the abandoned ship; at first the guard stopped me, but let me through when I muttered that I had left something behind and gave him a shilling. There in the darkness of the deathly quiet ship I cut you out of the wall and took you with me. Two weeks later I was taken on as fourth officer of the *Elefanta* bound for the East, where it was to stay, was given a cabin with the third officer, and you lay in a drawer: your double stood on the table. I saw you only when I came off watch, but you had changed: your face seemed more full of suffering. It made me sad to look at it. I never looked for long. I was scarcely ever alone. I would have liked to have you tattooed on my chest to have you with me always, but who could do it? I burnt your name into the skin of my armpit myself. At that time I did not know and did not dare to hope that you would one day read it. Years passed as we sailed up and down the Chinese coast.

Once we were berthed at the Upper Wharf in Shanghai waiting for orders, two hours away from the city by the twice-daily steam launch. By the first night we had lost our forward pay to the Russian drinking dens and after that stayed on board. It was winter – the cabins were badly heated, and it was lights out at nine-thirty. We shivered and bolted our meals in the chilly mess. At night we lay lonely in our bunks.

Each of us lived in his cabin as in a cell. We didn't play cards. In silence each of us drank the quantity of gin that he needed to keep going. The quantities varied greatly. I didn't need much. I just gazed at a piece of wood.

One evening, about ten minutes before lights out, an old ship-mate from the *Glenmore* dropped in to see me. We sulked and complained together as seamen do when they visit each other's ships in port: about the cold, the bad food, the fleecing that awaited us in port the moment we set foot on shore. This complaining brings a kind of consolation. One learns yet again that things are no better on other ships, sometimes even worse. Then came the warning signal with the light switched on and off that there were five minutes left. Jorgen suggested going on shore one last time: he knew a place in Chinatown that was cheap and reasonably honest. I was tempted for a moment, now the pitch-blank silence of the ship threatened, by the prospect of going to a house full of light, even if it was phoney red light. But I knew what it would come to, I hadn't got a damned sou, and refused. While we were talking he took the *London News* picture off the wall.

'Don't you even want to see Dolly? She's left the *St George* and she's here now.'

What was that? I grabbed my glass, emptied it, and lost consciousness. When I came round I seemed to have been gone for years. But Jorgen was still clutching the picture and kept repeating, 'It's her, I'm sure it's her.'

I gave a forced laugh. 'It was cut out of a magazine over a year ago, she was a countess or something, I think.'

'That's quite possible. Surely you know that if they can't get a shot of the duchess herself, they use a nice-looking dancing girl. That must be why all those dancing girls call themselves countess or baroness. No, a dancing girl can also turn into a sing song girl. It's Dolly who used to be at the *St George* and is now there,' Jorgen repeated stubbornly. 'Well, perhaps it's not her after all. Let's not go.'

But now I wanted to know. I retrieved the woodcut from a drawer. It was the first time I had shown you to anyone. Immediately the light went out and then it reappeared by the light of a struck match, more clearly than in full light. Jorgen stared at it. For a long while he was silent. Then he said, 'The spitting image, it's definitely her.'

I went up the stairs and Jorgen chased after me. 'Take it easy and stay below, it'll be an hour yet before the last launch goes. A sampan won't make it with this tide.' But I had already hailed one, the only one still lying in the churning water under the jetty, which charged a dollar for the crossing.

The old ferryman yanked us slowly across the broad current, sleet wafted into the deck shelter. Intermittently the lamp illuminated an arbitrary patch of the yellow water. We drifted badly off course and finished up three jetties from town.

Half an hour's walk. Half an hour in the tram. A rickshaw through the concessions. And a litter through Chinatown. It took hours, and I went through years of torment. In single file we negotiated alleys on the bouncing chairs, to the groans of the bearers amid the screech of the crowds pouring out of the open houses into the street. And all the way I was wondering: would it be you? And would it be over the bridge? No, for God's sake not that.

But it was over the bridge.

(White women, once in a house over the bridge, never return to European soil except to be buried.)

We crossed the zigzag bridge.

Jorgen urged the coolies on. Passing a few more narrow, dirty, winding alleys we emerged onto a dark square, unlit so that the pale red transparency in the windowless wall was the only light. Beneath it was a low door, unpainted, the letters half erased. The snow struck the side of the wall, slowly burying the beggars crouching there extending their hands to the late customers.

We pushed the door open. A grey-haired attendant was dozing on a chair. Four steep steps. A cold parlour, dreadfully squalid. An album on the dilapidated table. I flicked through the pages like a man possessed. One, two, three, twenty, thirty; you weren't there.

'What's wrong?' called Jorgen when he saw me slumped on my chair. Indeed, what was wrong? Was I sad or relieved that you were not there? Oh Larrios, I was sad, I wanted to find you and I had waited years. What did I care about where it was?

'She's not there,' I said hoarsely.

'Give me that book a minute. Here. You missed her. There she is, look.' So I had to find you! My hand hovered over number 39.

'Here, this one.' The old attendant shuffled off.

It took ages. Sometimes I jumped up ready to go. Then I sank back into my chair. Jorgen saw how on edge I was. He said in a tone of concern, 'Just as long as she's free. She'll be busy. It's just after Chinese New Year.' I groped in my right-hand pocket.

'Give me that!' There was a struggle. Then the attendant came down.

'Number 39. Can do.' I tried to get up, but could not leave the room. Jorgen accompanied me, calming me down and understanding nothing.

'Don't be a fool. Take a short time. I'll collect you in an hour.' I pushed open a door, tripped over a screen and behind it there you lay, Larrios, in a kimono that you opened when I entered.

I closed the robe around you, and sat down beside you. Stroked your blue hair, stammering your name. Perhaps you had forgotten your name, and thought I was drunk. You sat there staring. Then I said, 'Larrios, Burgos, Málaga.' And you started laughing and rattled off a string of places: 'Marseilles, Port Said, Colombo.' – Guilt, often disease. – Then your hard professional laugh again. But I did not laugh. You nudged me. I sat where I was. Then tears, lots of tears. Why? Was your professional pride wounded, Larrios? I'm inclined to think so. Because when I took my clothes off your face began to brighten. Did you think I was going to use you and then leave? In that case why would I have gone to such lengths to make you sad first?

It was very difficult. But it was even more difficult to make you understand that you must now take my clothes and my money and leave. Take the boat and wait for me in Manila. There you would be safe under American jurisdiction. And when you finally understood and agreed, as astonished as I had ever seen anyone, you first wanted me to take you and I think you were angry when I did not want to, when I rushed you into getting dressed and you only agreed after my solemn promise that in Manila I would have you for a year for free. I had a sneaking feeling that you had less in common with the old Larrios than the rough wooden portrait that I had of you. But I would find you again, Larrios, even if it meant doing what you asked. Having free use of you for a year – I would gradually learn to love you again. I would unearth you once more. How can anyone be so full of hope after eight years' roaming in search of a woman, after eight years of that life!

You were almost ready and I was about to slip on your kimono. But there was a knock at the door. You flinched and grabbed my arm, 'Not open, don't open'.

Oh, Larrios, this was nothing; stranger things happen than our dressing up. But you were frightened that you would not be able to get away now. I was happy at your fear, forgive me.

It was Jorgen, come to see where I had got to.

He saw at a glance what had to be done, but was worried about me.

But I said: 'I'll manage, quick, off you go, leave your overcoat here, Jorgen.' And they went. That was the third time; a hurried, hectic hour. The first time was a glance from a train, the second a night of exhausted sleep. And my wretched life hung from those three meetings like a broken-backed bridge on wrecked piers. For years. I lay on the sofa, calculating: now Jorgen is paying the brothel-keeper while you go on ahead, now you are getting into a chair, now you are out of Chinatown, thank God.

The door opened. An Irish sailor was admitted. He did not give me away. 'Splendid joke,' he said when I explained things and went next door.

But almost immediately a Chinese came in who did not find it a joke and made such a huge fuss that the brothel-keeper appeared with two henchmen and found me there. The two thugs grabbed me by the scruff of the neck and the elbows. The brothel-keeper went off and returned with two coolies carrying bamboo canes, stoves and tongs. Glowing coals were put into the stoves. They tied me up. The brothel-keeper said that I was under Chinese law here. He heated a pair of tongs himself. I determined not to make a peep. But when the tongs burned into my flesh, I let out a cry, controlled myself for a moment, but simply could not keep my mouth shut.

At that moment the door was kicked open and the Irishman I had just met, two other white men and all the women in the house forced their way into the room. One, two slashes with the knife and I was free again. The Irishman pushed me out of the door, the brothel-keeper and his assistants were unable to fight their way through the melee of women. Behind us we heard *'banzai, evviva, hurrah'*, we slammed the street door shut, and the Irishman was able to roll a heavy stone in front of it that he had pulled from the top of the wall. We ran, pushing coolies aside, turning as many corners as we could. Behind us we heard alarm gongs – we ran on between grinning yellow faces and swaying lanterns. There was no end to it, would we escape? In an hour's time the whole of Chinatown would be in uproar. We must be out of here before then. We stopped behind a dungheap; there was no one there yet. Dawn was beginning to break. Then three rickshaws approached after having dropped off some late customers at one of the houses. When they saw us they rushed towards us, placed the shafts right at our feet. Thank God, they knew nothing about the pursuit. 'The Bund' is the Irishman's curt instruction to the first of them, and in an unbelievably short time we had driven through a few alleys, out of the gate and were rolling down Edward Avenue, another world.

Where was I to find Jorgen? I first had to go into a pub with the Irishman and drink and drink to this crazy jape, this narrow escape. Finally he was blind drunk, half choking in gales of laughter and whiskies. I took him to his launch, my saviour, whom I would never see again.

Now to find Jorgen. Where might he be waiting for me? For the rest of the day I walked up and down the Bund, sometimes taking a break in the Russian tea rooms in the narrow wayside park when the flotsam and jetsam of the city and the ships met. The beach-combers, the starving Russians, the prostitutes who could no longer find work, the rickshaw coolies who could no longer run.

I sit there and wait. Is that Jorgen coming past? 'Larrios has gone, is out of it all,' I murmur to keep my courage up. Towards midnight I get up and make my way with sudden certainty to Alcazar – that's where I'll find Jorgen. He is there. Sitting in a corner with other Norwegians. He sees me, gets up, pushes me down onto a chair, pushes a glass towards me and I drink. He tells the others something. They laugh and smile in approval. I finally pluck up courage. 'Where did you leave her?' Jorgen grins. 'She didn't want to go at first. But she's already on board. The *Suzanna*. I know the captain. She's got a good cabin, sixty dollars. She may have to do a bit extra for it.'

Only now do I realise that she would have been fairly safe in the European quarter of Shanghai too. Why the tearing hurry? Now we are separated again. Why? I wanted her far, far away from this place.

Jorgen stared at me. 'Cheerio, in a few days she'll be with her compatriots. That's where you wanted her to go, wasn't it, she's bound to have someone there.'

How good that Jorgen said that. Because now I know why I wanted this. As long as she was in Shanghai she would be a prostitute. In Manila she'd be the Spanish woman from Burgos, from Málaga again.

'Do you know of a ship bound for there, Jorgen?' I said. Just like that first time I had no money left to join you. I gave every penny I had to pay for your ticket.

Jorgen peered into his glass. At last he said: 'The *Long Shan* goes there occasionally. That's the only one I know.'

I went back on board in the darkness, telling the sampan to wait. In a few minutes I had packed a chest, gave the watchman a dollar, slept the night on the Broadway, and signed on as quartermaster of the *Long Shan*.

In the afternoon we sail down the Yangtze. I stand on deck, pass the *Glenmore* with Jorgen on board, the *Elefanta* still in dock, half dismantled. I see no one and no one sees me on the deck of the *Long Shan*, sailing downriver, to meet Larrios. Past the battle cruisers, at anchor in the middle of the river. The Spanish one is small and dirty and has its flag at half mast. That makes me sad. Why?

*

We are sailing to meet Larrios. It will take months before we put into Manila. We call at Sebu, Mindanao, but never Manila or even Luzon. Otherwise I would have risked a cross-country journey from any port.

Why did we never have freight for Manila? Once we were on our way there but got caught in a typhoon, had to seek shelter and transfer the cargo.

And then I gave up and became what I had never been in my life, a passenger, just a deck passenger, and for three days sat among Chinese and Filipinos on a hatch, staring at Manila like a *haji* at Mecca. It stinks, the food is disgusting, the crew look at me sitting there with contempt. What did it matter! In my belt I had a hundred dollars. Better give them to Larrios than to a shipping company. And when we entered the Bay of Manila I felt like the governor, like Columbus.

Larrios, I was wondering where I might find you. You had to live. But I assumed that you would no longer live the same life, for my sake, for the sake of your miraculous escape. So what was left? You couldn't sew here, you'd probably lost the knack. Nor could you sit typing in an office. What is left for a woman who has no one and doesn't want to give herself to all-comers? I was firmly convinced I would find you on the dancefloor.

I started with St Anna, where there is a floor large enough for three hundred couples at a time. I sat there drinking whisky for three nights. I never saw you among the Filipino women, who keep their mantillas on when dancing, their arms with the protruding sleeves bent elegantly away from their bodies.

I continued my search in ever more obscure establishments where the clientele was more international.

By day I wandered around the old city and hid from the harsh light in the grey gloom of the cathedrals.

One Friday morning – I spent a long time wandering about – I went into San Pedro, just to find some quiet corner. And there, in the brightly coloured distance by the altar I saw you prostrate on your knees by a pillar and rushed to you, tried to embrace you, paying no heed to church or veil. But I found myself looking into a strange, alarmed face and fled from the echoing church as if I had seen a ghost. For days I was afraid to enter churches; fortunately there were also streets so narrow that they lay in shadow almost all day long. The Intramuros quarter is big but I passed through the same streets at least ten times. Every day. What was I still looking for? Had you not long since left, hidden yourself in some place I could not extricate you from so easily? Days passed. I walked through the streets muttering, feeling my way along vacantly with a stick, attracting looks, or I lay dozing against a harbour wall among beggars covered in sores swarming with flies, and paid-off sailors who were unable to find a new ship. Am I in the same situation? I don't know, I'm not going to try anymore, even if it means rotting here.

At night I slept in the godowns between sacks of tobacco or rice, or whatever. The coolies left me lying there out of pity.

One morning I was chased off early and wandered out of Manila at first light, to the area where country houses lie on low hills. I don't see them, my face is focused on the ground, following the path. Around a bend, I do not know why, I see a house on a green slope with wonderful lawns, pink and white against the blue. I cannot take my eyes off it.

After a while a pair of dogs start barking. Has someone set them on me?

No. They are kept on the leash by a woman, slim and dressed in a dark robe, one hand playing with a whip – the stance and face are hers.

It is almost unnervingly quiet; the two of us outdoors in the early morning, only a lawn between us, the blue sky above. No train dragging me past, no ship I belong on, no house imprisoning you.

There's no need to hurry. This is the one moment, the spot to which I have steered across almost every ocean.

Slowly I climb the path, you stand at the top and are looking somewhere, not at me. Don't you recognise me, Larrios? We were always in disguise, weren't we?

You are about to go back in the house. But a gesture of mine as I climb up forbids this. You release the dogs, but they scarcely move. One lies down immediately, the other circles you.

But the moment I approach you, so close I can look into your eyes, you are further away than you ever were when I sought you from sea to sea.

'Larrios. Don't you recognise me?'

'Can't you see my circumstances have changed, that I'm so…'

'Each time you were someone different. What does it matter? How I've searched. Let me rest.' And I tried to nestle against her. I'd seen her eyes, hadn't I?

She takes a step back.

'Don't you understand? You can't stay here like this.'

She points to me, to the house behind.

I understand: in that house is another owner, more powerful than the poor Chinese brothel-keeper, who lets her wander round freely.

'Come back tonight and I'll give you back the money for the boat, get dressed, come back and perhaps…'

It has taken less than two minutes, and in the space of a few words Larrios has died inside me – Larrios who has lived within me for years. How can one survive when it happens so quickly? It is true that I aged years as I went down the hill. Behind me, she called out something else, but it was over. I didn't look back.

There's no need to take my own life. Tonight, or in a few nights' time, as I lie in the crew's quarters of some nameless ship, a speck of dirt among other dirt, and night and sea surround the ship, won't it be just the same, especially if I never go ashore again and lie beneath the heavy timbers in the narrow cabin, with rotten wood against my head and feet and above me, won't it be the same as –

And if on the first night at sea I tie a stone to a piece of wood that for years was like a part of me and drop it from the forecastle: one, two, three, for ever – won't that be as good as a rope round my neck, or an iron grille round my feet?

Everything can go on as before. What has really changed?

My Black Sister

Cola Debrot

translated by Paul Vincent

The harbour of the Dutch Caribbean island began with a long channel that ended in a capriciously shaped bay; seen on a map a stalk with a bunch of flowers on it. The approach was so wide that quite large steamers could easily turn in it and so long that the ships could dock on both sides along the quays.

One afternoon, like so many tropical afternoons, a steamer was just turning in the harbour; small sloops were tugging cables that kept striking the surface of the water, as if invisible giantesses were skipping. A young man stood on the deck observing it all, and thought: Quite extraordinary. It's extraordinary enough that I'm called Frits Ruprecht, which to others must sound like two first names. And it's extraordinary that I've come back to this island, where I was born, because of my mother's and now my father's death, and maybe also because I'm sick of Europe, where one sees far too few black people. I'm glad I've enough money to last me a lifetime. I want to live with a black woman. I'll call her: my black sister. In Europe I hated those cold, pallid, fish-like faces with their total lack of brotherly or sisterly warmth.

Against the backdrop of the quay, lined with traditional Dutch pointed gables, a private motor launch came hurtling towards the big ship and – after turning in a wild arc – came alongside the ship's gangway. The *mulatto* who previously had been at the helm was now holding the little vessel close to the high side of the mail boat with a hook, near one of the jets pumping rhythmically out of the neighbouring bilge hole. A short, thick-set gentleman in grey shantung, wearing a straw hat, stepped from his motor launch onto the gangway, which he began slowly climbing. On reaching the top he was greeted by the captain and an individual dressed in white linen, with a tropical helmet on. Ruprecht watched. They formed a typical group for the tropics: a pith helmet, a straw hat, a uniform sleeve with three or four gold rings. The three chatted to each other, like people in a hurry, but still keen to gossip a little. They pulled amused faces, the captain in particular revealing deep crow's feet round the corners of his eyes. They bowed. Then the captain turned in the direction of Ruprecht and because of the distance shouted, 'Mr Ruprecht, these gentlemen would like to speak to you.'

Before Frits Ruprecht had realised exactly what was happening, the two men from the tropics were standing in front of him. The man in white, who was a little younger and had red veins in his face like those of a leaf, extended both hands to him:

'Of course you've changed a lot since you were last here fourteen years ago. I'm Dr Wellen.'

'I still remember you, doctor.'

The thick-set gentleman in grey shantung, whose yellowy-grey face he at first found rather repellent, having long since lost his familiarity with the effect of the tropics, kept his hands in Frits' as he talked, until their palms began to stick together:

'Of course I regret that I am unable to look after your physical welfare like our friend Dr Wellen, and nor am I the man for your spiritual welfare... ' At these last words he broke off, smiled shyly and looked straight ahead as if his conscience were pricking him, 'but your fortune is still my responsibility... '

'I'd imagined you as older, Mr Notary, that's why I didn't recognise you immediately.'

'No, young man, spare me the compliments, I'm an old man, I'll soon be joining your poor father.'

'I remember you often came over to our place to play whist. As a child I liked the chips best. Round and oblong, red and white, green and black.'

'Old memories... '

The notary held his forehead between his fingers, gave a short laugh and squeezed the top of Frits' arm as if examining his biceps.

'Let me begin, Frits Ruprecht, son of Alexander Ruprecht and Marie Antoinette Clémence Villeneuve, born 4 May 1902, by handing you this bunch of keys as a city once surrendered its keys to the victorious general. I have attached these things to them, rather like chips. It will help you tell them apart. I've noted on the chips what each of them belongs to: the house in town, the coach house, which incidentally you'll be shocked to find is terribly run down; the house on the plantation and, as you know, we still call a plantation a kunuku here. So the key to the gate of the kunuku is also included. Anyway, they're all labelled precisely. So here are your keys. It's hot on board this ship. I won't make any long speeches. I hope you'll call on my services as your poor father did.'

'Thank you, Mr Notary.'

'Of course you'll be coming with me now. You can have a bite to eat with us first, see my wife, and Tonia, whom you of course won't remember.'

'Yes, I expect she'll have grown into a fine girl in those fourteen years.'

'Yes, a fine girl. That's the word for her. After that you can have my car and Wansitu for today. Am I not making myself clear? Wansitu is my chauffeur.'

'It's very kind of you, Mr Notary. I hope you won't mind if I don't accept your offer. I'd like to see everything with my own eyes, do everything for myself.'

'What are you driving at? I'm not as young as I was. The moment people start behaving oddly, I can't keep up with them.'

'I'd just like to go and get the old Ford that's in the coach house and that you wrote to tell me is still in working order. I'd like to drive it to the kunuku. I'll manage. I remember it all exactly: I was sixteen when I was last here.'

'This is a bit awkward. My wife is expecting you. Besides, I thought you'd be moving into a hotel first. You'd be completely free. You could relax.'

'Oh, please don't take it amiss, it may be better for me to be alone for these first few days.'

'I understand, I understand, my boy, but at least come with me in my launch.'

The doctor, who had gone off for a moment, returned and joined in the conversation.

'One last little medical formality. You feel quite well, don't you, Frits?'

'Disgustingly well, sometimes I feel a complete animal.' They laughed. Frits still had to make all kinds of arrangements about his luggage. He crammed the essentials into his briefcase, and rejoined the notary. They walked slowly down the gangway. Ruprecht warned himself to be careful.

Above them, bent over the railing, the captain and the doctor were waving. The doctor put his mouth to the captain's ear as if telling a smutty joke that no one else must hear.

'Quite the little lord, cost his father thousands, won't be long before the rest is squandered, down the drain, up in smoke... '

The captain nodded and giggled, displaying his crow's feet.

Frits was to leave the boat at a small jetty, where the bright green water broke into a rocking motion and splashed against the low jetty.

'Can I leave you to make your own way, Frits?'

'I hope I'll be able to look after myself,' replied Frits with a laugh.

The notary answered, though with his thoughts already elsewhere: 'I'm sure you will. You look as if you've spent your whole life in Paris. I was there once too, long ago: Folies Bergère, Moulin Rouge, Claridge Hotel.' And with a laugh he added, 'In Paris one sees plenty of types like you. I don't know myself what I mean. But all the best, my boy, and if you need to know anything, come and see us, and you'll be able to see my wife and Tonia, who, as you yourself said, has grown into a fine girl.'

The old man and the young man shook hands. With a well aimed step Frits moved from boat to shore. The snow-white launch leapt forward again into the harbour, where one could see the stern of the steamship revolving like a huge billboard bearing its name and home port.

Frits stood all alone on the island of his birth, which he had not seen for so many years. The first emotion was pure rapture. His father was dead, his mother too, but these awful facts did not plunge the young man into insurmountable gloom. For him they were the undercurrent of melancholy that gave life a fatalistic colour; like an intoxicated sleepwalker, now virtually all has been lost, one feels that all is permitted and that life has nothing to offer but the weirdest adventures. Frits Ruprecht was determined to have his weird adventure: those would-be interesting white women in Passy or the ski resorts, in The Hague or at Wimbledon, *je m'en fous et je m'en fous pas mal.* What I want is my black sister. No more idle talk. Blackness and devotion.

This cheerful impulse inevitably gave way to a much gloomier one. Frits was immediately seized by the feeling that the best thing would be to commit hari-kiri on the spot, as he stood there alone on the jetty, with the imminent prospect of having to strike out into territory whose every nook and cranny had come back to him with crystal clarity. Nothing good was to be expected from something that left so little scope for ignorant fantasizing. This island, this remote corner of the world, still consisted of two parts: an Eastern and a Western half, divided by a harbour that cut like a deep sheath into the narrow island. One road led from the harbour to the westernmost tip, and one road from the harbour to the easternmost point. In both the Western and the Eastern part the road was lined on both sides by plantations of varying size. There was only one obvious difference: the road was bordered in the Western part by cactuses and in the Eastern part by agaves. At nightfall, in the very short tropical dusk, one could sometimes see a parrot perched on the top of a long thin cactus stalk: motionless, like an idol, while pink patches of the gruesomely bloody setting sun coloured the landscape of bare hills so strangely that it reminded Frits not only of the Western landscape of the island, but also of the ball gown and the body of a *femme de trente ans* he had kissed one evening as they

stood beneath the scent of chestnut trees somewhere in Europe...
These things were impossible to decide: did I kiss her so deeply
because she looked like Sylvia Sydney, whom I know only from
films, or because she was wearing a ball gown in the colours the
distant landscape assumed at dusk?

The Ruprecht plantation was in the Western part. He only knew
the Eastern part because as a boy he had often had to stay there,
with an uncle, an aunt, or at least a distant cousin. All the whites on
the small island were related by either blood or marriage. The black
coachman Pedritu would take him in the tilbury to the uncle, the
aunt or the distant cousin. In his children's suit with knickerbockers
he had bumped along for hours beside Pedritu, who told him fairy-
tales, about spiders, about princesses that sing in the sky, about the
ghost that appears as a white donkey with a blue star between its
upright ears; the black driver tried to reassure him, determined at all
costs to distract the small boy, as he started whining about his
trousers that were sticking to his bottom, occasionally cuddling up
to the coachman and whispering:

'Pedritu, I'm getting so frightened. It's all different here.'

Frits knew better now: East or West, it was all the same. It was just
that the agaves gave the landscape a different character, which was
precisely what alarmed the little boy. Not the agaves themselves. You
could make wonderful mischief with the agaves. Using a sliver of glass
or an old rusty nail that one found on the ground somewhere, you
could carve the words that boys in Holland chalk on fences and
toilets. You could write all sorts of things. You could even bare your
heart, that most vulnerable of human organs, and reveal: I love Lydia
or Jane or Carlota.

After a few days a scab grew over them and there were clear
words on the green leaf as if written on parchment. When the agaves
were in bloom one saw humming birds quivering around the blos-
soms like big butterflies...

What names would Frits Ruprecht carve now if he were standing in front of a blank fresh-green agave leaf, rusty nail in hand?
Probably he wouldn't know. Ruprecht could not stand here on this
jetty any longer, drugging himself with memories. He must act. He
walked rapidly down the main street of the town. Occasionally a

black woman would stop and look round at the young man who was moving much too fast for the tropics; she would call another black woman, stretched out on a step for her siesta: 'Who's that? Is he a stranger? Or someone from the island perhaps?' Occasionally Ruprecht would reply in the local *patois*. This would delight the women and they would shout back, cackling with laughter. Ruprecht walked on. Along the wide street stood a disparate assortment of houses: great mansions, with galleries and balconies running the whole length of the house fronts, alternated with very ordinary dwellings that were more like shanties. The shanties were liveliest; in them black women lay combing and cutting each other's hair; their frizzy hair was oiled and pulled taut; the woman doing the pulling took the opportunity to inflict pain; the woman whose hair was being pulled responded with a string of oaths in which the Virgin Mary had a particularly hard time of it. The big houses, however, stood there in complete silence, with all their shutters closed. Ruprecht suddenly remembered that a young girl had once stood between two pillars of one of these galleries: rather tall and skinny, with quite large feet; but also with bright blue eyes and blonde hair. She stood between the two pillars and smiled as silently and cruelly as only girls of fourteen can. After all these years she was still mocking Frits Ruprecht. Pain went through his heart, another old wound had been opened. At that moment the slats of blinds snapped open. Ruprecht watched closely. Between the chinks of the blinds he could see part of a human face, the part that remains unveiled in the women of a harem: eyes, the bridge of the nose and just a little of the cheeks... Probably a lonely white woman was now peering at the stranger she could not place... What a melancholy thought: 'A woman of thirty, who is now peering at me, and a fourteen-year-old who once laughed at me; it would be too stupid for words if they turned out to be one and the same person.' But coincidence was not as neat as that. The only real coincidence was that at that precise moment he spotted a petrol station, with yellow Shell pumps; there probably wouldn't be any petrol in the coach house. There were Goodyear tyres hanging up, and Dunlops, and the Michelin Man, the same as everywhere else. And car parts: spark plugs, lights, carburettors. The man who came towards

Ruprecht was an American in shirtsleeves, without a collar, a belt holding up his trousers around his heavy midriff; his face was a white oval.

'Can I have two cans of petrol?'

'Are you going to carry them with you?'

'No. Surely you must have someone?'

The man did not answer, but stepped outside a moment and called something into the street. Soon a black man was standing there with a wheelbarrow into which the two cans of petrol were loaded. Ruprecht called to the black man in the local *patois*:

'Just follow me.'

On hearing his own language the black man swamped Ruprecht with questions about where he came from.

'I knew your father well. I often fetched petrol for him too. Come to that, I often did his shopping. And I took letters to the post office.'

They both laughed. There were times when Ruprecht's father, seized with fear of heaven knows what, suffered from a veritable writing mania; and in addition there was his pile of business correspondence. This laugh also marked the end of the conversation. Ruprecht stopped answering. You could hear the single wheel rolling along; when the two cans knocked against each other, they rattled briefly.

Finally Ruprecht turned into a small side street full of nothing but shanties, pervaded by a sweetish banana smell. The black women sat on stools against the walls of the shanties. They shouted their questions at the black man, who, somewhat intimidated by Ruprecht's silence, answered only reticently. Still, it was enough, and the black women shouted out loud, 'The young master's come back, the young master's come back.' Frits had a special significance for these women: he was the landlord of the neighbourhood.

The street ended where the Ruprecht property began. The big house itself stood slightly off-centre: it was a square building, with a pyramid-shaped roof; only on one side had the house had an extension built on, which, however, remained single-storey and at first-floor level was covered with a half saddle roof. This square white house with closed shutters everywhere and peeling light-green paint, reminded him of a mausoleum; not for all the world would Frits Ruprecht have opened up this house; for him his dead parents rested in this house rather than in the cemetery that he would shortly be racing past – the Ford should still be able to do 40 kph; his dead parents were lying side by side in the closed house, eyes wide open and staring at the ceiling. He would not be intruding into this house for the time being.

The property consisted of various sections. From the main gate, where the street with the cloying smell ended, small paths led between agaves and anglos (the poppies of the tropical island) to the house; to the bleaching field beyond; to the coach house nearer the main building; to the detached cottage occupied by the old seamstress who, despite the constant drought, grew flowers: velvety dahlias, roses you could smell, camellias and amaryllises grown mainly to be looked at. In the grounds, besides the agaves and the small yellow anglos on the ground, one saw red bunches blooming on the karawara trees. Close to the house a great tamarind spread its crown into the sky; at the bottom of the bark of the massive tree Ruprecht saw black stains: the blood shed by the scores of sheep and goats that Pedritu had slaughtered here over the years. Ruprecht remembered as if it were yesterday the short, violent convulsions of the animal as its jugular vein emptied in a spurt; with a single stroke of the sharp knife, which was first whetted at length on the grindstone, the animal's life was taken...

Blood, this life is blood... At that moment a single tamarind dropped from a bough and fell silently to the ground; the only sound he could hear was the squeak of the wheelbarrow. Ruprecht stood in front of the coach house. Pressing his key briefly into the yale lock he was able to open the doors to the side like the pages of a very heavy book. The silent black man, who occasionally scratched his head, helped him. The notary was right: this coach house was terribly dilapidated: his father must have neglected it for years; even from outside one could see that the planks, which had never been repainted, were rotting away. He looked through the open door at the back of the old Ford's bodywork; one could clearly see the number plate spattered with dried mud and, through the back window, the steering wheel, the dashboard... To the side of the vehicle, against one wall, a plank lay on two stone blocks; that was where Pedritu had slept, back in the days of the tilbury... Grubby playing cards lay on the ground, red diamonds and black spades, reminding him, like the notary's chips, of the excitement of long-forgotten games. There was also a halter hanging from a roof beam, recalling the era of carriages. Ruprecht started for a moment: he caught sight of three rusty petrol cans against the wall. He tapped them with the toe of his shoe: they were not empty. This was the petrol his father had not been able to use before he died.

The tank was filled with the petrol he had brought. A few minutes later he was at the wheel, out on the country road. Cactuses to the left and right. An arid, undulating landscape. The few trees on the top of slopes or hills were small and what is more completely bowed by the north-easterly trade wind that has blown since time immemorial, one way, one way... After a few kilometres the landscape kept bursting open into larger and smaller groves of coconut palms with their flapping leaves. The cactus border alternated for a while with a whitewashed wall and on one of the hills a white country house would loom up. It was at just such a country house that in a few hours' time he would end his journey at the wheel. Because of the many ups and downs in the road, he was constantly jerking the steering wheel to the left and right. Groups of black women, carrying tubs or baskets of fish, melons and vegetables into town, leapt aside and squeezed against the border when they heard the car approaching. He saw them from a long way off; they carried their loads loose on their heads, hands on their swaying hips. As the car approached they clutched at their heads, broke into a run, laughing like fleeing black nymphs. The dust thrown up by the car obscured them. In the mirror in which he tried to catch a last glimpse of the women, he saw nothing but yellowy pink dust that gradually lifted, like smoke after a gunshot.

Frits Ruprecht braked, stopped the car and got out. He had come to a spot where the road widened into a kind of village square. There was a little white church with a saddle roof surmounted by a white stone cross, definitely too ostentatious for the surrounding poverty. Almost as ostentatious as the policeman in white trousers, blue jacket and a blue canvas helmet resplendent with the arms of the House of Orange in copper and the motto: *je maintiendrai*. The policeman, truncheon in hand, was posted in front of the only mansion in the village.

Small black boys gathered round the Ford, jostling to look inside at the dashboard. Elsewhere, by the brown clay huts with their reed roofs, a donkey tethered to a stake pushed into the ground, let its head hang low; one ear and the skin of one leg twitched sporadically. Frits Ruprecht walked over to the policeman.

'Is the district officer in?'

The policeman touched his helmet.

'Yes, sir, shall I announce you?'

'That won't be necessary, I'll do it myself.'

Frits went up to the closed door of the house the policeman was standing in front of. Used to European ways, he first looked for the bell, but then rapped on the wood with his knuckles. A black woman opened the door. Ruprecht called over her shoulder:

'Are you there, Karel?'

'Who is it?' said a distant voice.

'It's me, Karel… Frits Ruprecht.'

'Come in, old chap, come in.'

Following the voice Ruprecht went through the house, his steps echoing in the emptiness of the rooms, which, as quite often happens in the tropics, had been only sparsely furnished. Apart from that this house, oddly enough, was very little different from any house one might call at in The Hague, probably a whim of a government contractor unable to keep his homeland out of his thoughts. Finally Frits passed through the back door into a small yard, most of which was taken up with a bleaching field. Items of clothing, still damp, were spread out and weighted down with large heavy stones. The voice called, 'Here I am.' The man he had called Karel was sitting in a wooden summerhouse, a small shed, with one wall removed, so that one saw the man seated inside, the way a painter would portray someone in a room. He was sitting in a wicker chair, holding a well-thumbed novel; on the wicker table were a green bottle and a pair of old weathered glasses; next to them were several coconuts cut open.

'Well I never, it's Frits. Have a seat. Like a rum and coconut milk? Even a European won't turn his nose up at that. Must be quite a life, over there in Europe. But to experience for yourself, not to hear someone else blathering on about it. So I'd prefer it if you'd down your rum and coconut milk, take your hat and leave. There's not much news anyway.'

'I haven't come to tell you anything. I just wanted to see you for a moment. I suddenly remembered that my father wrote me, four years ago, that you had been made district officer here. District officer is something like an American sheriff, isn't it?'

'Don't get me wrong, Frits. I'm not upset at your turning up here unannounced. Anyway, I'd heard from the notary that you were coming back this year. But why come sailing in like a ghost?'

'Karel, I hope you've not become frightened of ghosts in the meantime... Do you remember when we used to go hunting? For rabbit, ground doves, wild duck, parakeets, parrots...'

'I've got all the time in the world to remember it all, I haven't sauntered through every city in Europe. That's why I'm asking you: stay a ghost. Don't go on about the years since we last saw each other. Nothing wears me out and gets up my nose as much as people who are forever telling you their life story.'

'Come on, cheer up, Karel old man – or "White Devil", as the blacks used to call you. Pour me the rum, with coconut milk. I won't burden you with ten years of Europe. Come to that, I think you're overrating it as a continent, greatly overrating it.'

'But you've got to admit that anything good one were to say about the clod of earth that I live on, would, to put it mildly, be over-rating it too.'

'I don't know, perhaps I'm not completely responsible for my actions, but two months ago I felt so miserable in some corner or other of Europe, that on the spur of the moment I packed my bags and screamed, "Here I sleep in the arms of fish, their fins slapping against me in mockery. I want a black woman..." Anyway it's not such a bad idea, now my parents are dead and I've no one else, to take things to the limit.'

'Drink up, Frits, I'll pour you another, you may have missed this now and then in Europe: rum and coconut milk. You're all het up. No one is going to stop you having a black woman in this country. For all I care three black women, though I've only two myself. But the fact that you're shouting about it, proves it goes deeper. Talking of deep…'

Karel broke off in mid-sentence. He slid his elbows across the table, so close to Frits that Frits looked at him with some astonishment:

'You think of course that this book is some kind of thriller I'm reading to kill time out here in the sticks, an Edgar Wallace or an Ivans, and that I'm an alcoholic as well. Well, it isn't a thriller. It's Shakespeare; I'd never read *Othello* before.'

Ruprecht's eyes nearly popped out of his head. He did not immediately take in what Karel said, and actually thought he'd misheard. He was even more puzzled by Karel's fixed stare and the sudden change in his tone.

'What on earth are you saying, Karel? Forgive me, I sometimes have hallucinations these days, and hear absurd words and voices.'

Karel looked him straight in the face with his pale blue eyes and his lips slowly parted and closed again: '*Othello*, by Shakespeare.'

Frits' face drained in astonishment. It was surprising enough in itself that Karel should be reading Shakespeare in this desolate village square, but what surprised him even more was the tone in which he was informed of this, a tone midway between resolve and hostility; not the slightest trace remained of the voice that had initially sounded indifferent but not unfriendly. Frits would have most liked to shout, 'Come on, cheer up!' but this time he could not bring himself to utter the cordial words. He sat there looking at the face of the district officer. Slowly a smile spread across the red face, at once cold and complacent. It was absurd to assume that Karel was trying to insult him. Nevertheless Frits got to his feet, pushing back the chair. He stood facing Karel, who sat there motionless. Karel, who had once been his friend, but whose behaviour was now incomprehensible and ambivalent. Perhaps life's horrors finally rendered everyone less than fully responsible for their actions; Ruprecht put out his hand hesitantly as if saying goodbye for the last time to a former friend. Karel put his hand in Frits' like a dead bird; as he did so he averted his eyes, not because he could not bear the other's gaze, but as if disdaining to give Frits another look. Frits walked slowly through the echoing house; step after step resonated with a sound that seemed to exist independently of Frits. Outside, the policeman touched his helmet. Still pondering the bewildering conversation, he started the car with the awkward crank handle. Leaving a cloud of smoke in its wake the Ford disappeared, stared at by the little black boys with their swollen poverty-stricken bellies.

When the district officer heard the door close behind Ruprecht, he continued staring vacantly into space for a moment. Suddenly he burst out laughing. Alone in the little summerhouse he slapped his thighs with pleasure. He poured himself another rum and coconut milk and reached for his dog-eared book; not *Othello* by the great English writer, but a detective story by Edgar Wallace, in which a Chinese who had studied at Oxford and had a spiteful nature, tried to seduce a British girl. He immediately closed the book again and put it back on the table. Yawning and stretching, he shouted a few words in the local *patois* that sounded impossibly crude on the lips of this white man whose red face bulged, as with some alcoholics. The words were repeated loudly by a black woman's voice in the house, just as in Africa messages are conveyed through the living bush telegraph. Immediately afterwards the policeman appeared in front of the summerhouse.

'Look here, Toontshi,' the district officer began, 'we've had nothing to do for ages. This evening we must go out on patrol, just for a change. What if we set up an observation post near the house of that Mr Ruprecht who was just here? Yes, that was Mr Ruprecht. I don't expect anything will happen – he was always one for talking big. I really caught him out just now. Toontshi, don't ever read *Othello* by Shakespeare! That fine young gentleman has time on his hands, so he just throws up everything because he wants a black woman. Well, you and I have got nothing but black women, and we don't think it's such a big deal. Let him have his black woman. His Othella. We may have a bit of a laugh tonight.'

The policeman's grey-black face with the mongoloid cheekbones broke into a smirk. He enjoyed hearing one white man sounding off about another; for his benefit justice was driving a wedge between people who regarded him as inferior. He quickly made a few gestures and spoke a few words indicating that he would be happy to come out on patrol with the district officer and recommended that the district officer climb over the fence of the plantation at a particular spot and follow a particular path to the house where they could easily take cover in the dark. A string of picturesque names of paths, woods and hills flew from his mobile mouth. Chopping motions of the hand in the air served to provide the connection and linked these names to a strategic plan.

'Upon my word,' said the district officer, interrupting him, 'you're just like a Chinese. Do you know who your father was by any chance? Yes? Well it never ceases to amaze me that he wasn't Chinese. There's something of a black Chinese about you.'

The policeman burst out laughing. But the district officer's face remained motionless. In fact, the policeman saw the silent smile spread across the red face that he always took as a sign to withdraw.

Dusk was already falling as Frits Ruprecht fiddled with the padlock on the gate of the *Miraflores* plantation. Behind him the Ford seemed to have been borne up into space by the vague colours of the approaching night. The hilly terrain, with the few gnarled trees was cloaked in the transparent green membrane of the evening that would soon thicken into black night.

It was the old black steward who came in response to the noise of the padlock. He came and stood directly opposite Frits, on the other side of the gate. Frits was annoyed that old Wantsho did not recognise him at once, but seemed to look right through him with eyes staring blindly into the distance. The blackness of his face contrasted sharply with the whiteness of his shirt, like black sealing wax on a white envelope; over his trousers he wore a tight-fitting apron. His frizzy grey hair was so fluffy it seemed the wind might blow it away.

'Don't you recognise me, Wantsho! I'm Frits Ruprecht.'

'Mr Frits!'

The padlock was unhooked and the two halves of the gate opened inwards, while old Wantsho talked and apologised.

'Forgive old Wantsho, he's growing old, his eyes are getting weak and Mr Frits has come so unexpectedly at nightfall.'

'The notary couldn't tell you much, of course.'

'No, only that you were coming, some time this year.'

Frits was back at the wheel. But he did not put his foot down at once. He looked around gloomily. Head bowed, Wantsho stood to one side of the gate, with the heavy iron padlock in his frail old black hands. For a moment Frits also bent his head and looked down at the steering wheel, the paint of which had been worn off at the sides by the hands of his father and a driver he had not known. Then his eyes followed the contours of the landscape again. Chalky white, like a scream in the transparent green evening, the lavish white-washed walls stretched into the distance, dating from a time when slaves built interminable stretches the moment there was no other work for them, no lime or charcoal to burn, no coconuts to clamber up the tall trunks for, no stock to tend, no irrigation work needing attention... The walls on both sides of the gate were also white-washed, as were those bordering the drive.

Closer to the entrance were the fronts of the outbuildings, like great white banners from which the ephemeral words had been washed by streaming rain. In the distance, on the top of the hill, he saw the dim shape of the house on its broad stone terrace.

At this distance, because of its whiteness and the shape of its roof, it was reminiscent of an outsize tent, abandoned by people who had hurriedly moved on. In stormy weather its white canvas sides might have heaved like the wings of a huge bird.

Frits put his foot down, and the car surged forward up the drive. The steward pushed the gate shut behind him. He had only a vague memory of how to get to the garage, a former stable; he knew the general direction, but had forgotten the location. Now he realised that some things can sink into oblivion in fourteen years. It was absurd getting upset with Wantsho for not recognising him at once; even the notary would not have given him such a warm welcome without the captain's help. Frits drove slowly, edging his front wheels along the path. Wantsho was already there with the doors wide open when he arrived at the garage.

'You'd better tell them at the house that I've arrived. I'll lock up myself, I've got the keys from the notary.'

He sat and listened to the final judder of the engine as it stopped and then got out. Reluctantly. As the door slammed shut behind him, he had the feeling he was heading for an uncertain future, now he was about to re-enter the house where he had lived for so many years with his mother and father. They had repeatedly insisted that he come back and visit the island where he had spent his childhood. His mother had died years ago and, a month or so back, his father... His mind empty of thoughts, he leaned against the car, one foot on the running board... His mother... His father... Sometimes they appeared in his mind's eye, so clear, so alive that it startled him. Sometimes too they were just abstractions, names. He asked himself why he had come here the very first day. He wondered if he would stay here tonight. He could still go back to town. Move into a hotel as the notary had advised him. Then he would be able to look out from a balcony over the harbour where the light from the portholes would now be sparkling on the water. He could even spend a last night on board, in the familiar cabin. Slowly he closed the garage. Outside it was completely dark now. He walked slowly up the drive, but as he was about to climb the steps up to the terrace, he felt an urge to turn back and retreat as fast as his legs could carry him. Deep within him an old, dying voice lamented, 'Your mother's sitting in the dark on the terrace in a rocking chair... you can't see her... it's the sound of rocking and the scent of your mother that guide you... then you bump into the rocking chair... you touch your mother's dress... you feel your way round the lace collar at her neck... your mother holds out her hand to you... you play with the hand... and you twist one ring that was not, and the other that was her wedding ring...'

It was poignant remembering the hand he had once played with in the dark, and had sometimes brought to his lips, before giving one of the fingers a strangely playful bite. In his memory he re-experienced the way his mother laughed happily, but still pulled her hand away. The child pressed its face against its mother's, which returned the pressure. Just as playful, but issuing from an excess of tenderness, was the buzzing sound they both produced from deep down in their chests, without parting their teeth.

All that was long ago. Now he was walking across an empty terrace. He would no longer bump into a chair on which a young woman was slowly rocking. This brought with it a feeling of immense, almost nauseous emptiness, as if he were plunging from one void into another.

There was light coming from the house. Old Wantsho stood in

the doorway and looked at Frits, his blind eyes staring into the distance. The man did not take his eyes off Frits, and Ruprecht stared back with a frown. For the second time old Wantsho had annoyed him. The steward turned round and bowed.

'Good night, Mr Frits.'

What did the man want? He was probably getting past it. As Frits stood there lost in thought, he heard the rustle of a passing skirt, heard a woman welcome him with the official formula: 'Welcome to *Miraflores*, Mr Frits. I'll make some supper for you.'

'Fine,' Ruprecht had answered, staring after the old black man until he had disappeared completely into the darkness. Then he went into the house. It was like the opening of giant floodgates: reality and memory, fighting for precedence, poured over him. First he imagined himself back in the loft that he used to reach as a child by clambering up a ladder and clumsily opening a trapdoor with his head and hands... A maze of rafters and beams, from which bats hung by their claws, heads downwards. Motionless. But at the first impact of feet on the floor they started swaying. The ghostly creatures swayed like wisps of black cotton wool.

Next, it was the orderly plan of the interior that stunned him. He felt cheated. For all those years in Europe he had lived with figments of his imagination. The plan of the house bore scarcely any relation to the complicated, half-lit conception he had formed of it, those countless times he had recalled it, at night, when he could not sleep, half upright in bed, hugging his knees and staring into the dark, or during the day, stretched out in a sunny wood, with a handkerchief over his face and mosquitoes buzzing around his ears. Back then these two interior walls, which now seemed simplicity itself, had struck him as something mysterious. They ran parallel to the long side of the house and divided the space into a narrow front section, a narrow back section and a wider middle section. This middle section was in turn divided into three: his parents' bedroom on the left; the room where he himself used to sleep on the right; and in the middle the living room. The mystery was heightened by the arched openings made in the wall of the living room to the front and back of the house. Light streamed through them as if into an old abandoned church. The pillars of the arches rested on a thick low wall no more than knee-high, so that the small boy could easily scramble up under the arches and read his children's books. Frits rubbed his eyes to dispel the persistent phantoms. In his imagination the play of light under the arcades had created the unreal labyrinth that had gradually come to replace reality.

Frits stood dithering on the threshold between the front of the house and the living room, where there were no arcades or walls. Something prevented him from entering the living room. The sheen on this threshold, distributed unequally over the cement floor like the gloss on an animal's fur, was dazzling, almost intimidating, representing in his imagination a kind of gate dividing two worlds. Had the life gone out of the architecture together with the human faces whose expressions had changed as capriciously as the light in the arches of the arcades? In the living room it was always his father and mother or white relatives that he met. In the narrow front and back sections of the house a faint scent of black people always hung in the air – a scent that in Europe he often felt homesick for. The scent of the housekeeper, the steward or others who came to speak to his father. His father would talk to them at the door, or take them to the room at the front corner of the house.

The ends of the front and back of the house were partitioned off to make rooms designed for some special purpose. So the far left of the front of the house was turned into the kitchen, where smoky patches resembled the continents and where the black women some-times bustled about their work, and sometimes lay asleep on mats without moving a muscle. The bathroom and the former house-keeper's bedroom were created in the same way. As a child, when these rooms were locked, he had suspected that all kinds of things were going on behind the thin door panels, and occasionally had even pounded on the panels with his fist. Also at the front of the house was the room where his father used to deal with his corre-spondence when he was on the plantation. This room had made a deep impression on Frits. Probably the three-masted ship in full sail in a bottle would be hanging there, and the typewriter that had once given him the fright of his life: he had pressed a key and the carriage had shot from one end to the other with a loud bang. The typewriter would be standing there under its cover as if shrouded in mourning.

(In Holland a relative's suggestion that he wear a black mourning armband had made him feel almost physically sick.) In his father's study too the rifles must also still be leaning against the wall, the ones he took hunting with Karel, who was now district officer and who seemed to bear him a grudge for some reason he could not fathom.

But it wasn't just the district officer, it was the whole island that bore a grudge against him. He had come back to his country empty-handed, and so must wander down empty roads, through empty rooms and past people whose hearts remained empty of warmth towards him. He would have preferred to avoid the roads, the rooms and the people, just as he wanted no part of the house in town. That was why he dithered on the gleaming cement of the threshold: he would rather not have entered the living room. He was overcome by intense fear when a power stronger than himself drove him inside. The light given by the dim paraffin lamps at the front and back of the house and by the bright hanging lamp in the living room spread in circles of varying size over the floors and walls. The circles rotated past or intersected each other, and together with the deep shadows in the arches of the arcades, the segments of brighter or fainter light formed a huge luminous flower-head. Frits felt as if he were stepping into this flower-head of light, and at the same time into an ambush, something insubstantial, a gaping hole in space. His eyes searched for something to hold on to in this vacuum and seized on the door of the room to his left. This was where his parents had once slept. He had sometimes charged in there early in the morning and surveyed himself in his mother's dressing-table mirror, before cuddling up to her. By that time his father was already roaming the hills of the plan-tation, sometimes on horseback, on the timid bay called Boulanger, sometimes on foot with an axe in his hand to cut back cactuses and vines... 'My parents are still asleep behind those doors, my father, my mother,' cried a deafening voice within him... The voice echoed outside of him too. Almost without hesitating, Ruprecht leapt for the door and thrust it open. He glimpsed a light in the dressing-table mirror. But at the same moment someone or something with glowing eyes leapt back at him out of the darkness, grabbing him by the shoulders, and screaming in his ears. Deathly pale, he slammed the door shut again. He broke into a sweat of panic. Objects seemed to

be electrically charged – whenever he touched anything he felt a
shock. But then he came to his senses. This was getting out of hand.
Something was wrong, he wasn't completely responsible for his
actions, he was in an overexcited state. He must put such weird
adventures out of his head, what mattered most was to calm down.
A man must resist his own impulses.

It was only to pretend to himself that he felt secure that he
strolled so casually into the back section of the house. The door
knob turned with a creak in his grasp and the door blew open like a
shred of cloth in a hurricane; the back door was on the north side
and took the full force of the trade wind... For a moment Frits felt
attacked by the wind. The he got used to it and let the cool breeze
blow through his hair.

He looked out into an impenetrable blackness. Gradually his
eyes adjusted to it, but still he could distinguish nothing except by
its degree of blackness or simply by its sound. Only in the distance
could he see a few lines of light fanning out to sea, between the dark,
high arms of the rocky shore. The north coast of the island was so
inaccessible that the little bay he could see from here served as a
private playground for Frits and his friends, white and black, boys
and girls. Among them was Karel, who later went hunting with him
and today had proffered a hand like a dead bird. Also among them
was the girl cousin whose memory had caused him such pain that
afternoon in town. She stood between the pillars with her skinny
body and her oversized feet, but also with her bright blue eyes and
golden hair, and she laughed at him. Whenever they played on the
plantation too she had always laughed at him. She adored every
game dreamed up by Karel, with his eyes the pale blue of forget-
me-nots. She even pouted pretentiously at the beautiful shells with
their pink insides that Frits found on the beach of the little bay,
throwing the hair that blew forward back over her shoulders with a
spiteful gesture. No, she had cared little for him. They had played
over there too, where the fans of coconut and date palms rustled.
The occasional flash of light, from heaven knows what centuries-
distant star, struck the metallic leaves. The rush of the sea mingled
with the rustling of the leaves, before freeing itself again, so that the
two motifs could also be heard separately... The rushing, rustling

music awakened the memory of another fourteen-year-old girl... A feeling of gratitude welled up in Frits Ruprecht's heart towards his black companion Maria, who as it were protected him from his little cousin and in turn thought all of Karel's games really boring and preferred even Frits' silliest suggestions.

Here and there in the garden, where the coconut and date palms towered high above the clumps of mango and medlar trees, there were moss-covered stone benches, built in the days of slavery with no other purpose than to enable the various Elizabeths, Virginias, and Carolinas to listen to the rustling of the palm wood, the rhythmical friction of the fans, the periods of breathless silence, the distant cracking of a twig. Little Frits had thought up the game: clambering onto the old stone benches and sitting there, just sitting next to each other. His cousin of course thought it was too silly for words and ran off with Karel. For minutes Frits sat there with Maria and together they counted how many times they heard a woodpigeon coo in the distance. An intimate cooing, from deep in the throat.

Frits remembered this young black girl vividly. She had the kind of black skin one scarcely ever found among the largely mixed-race population of the island. But there was something very special about her: the shape of her head, her nose, and her lips were those of a white, not a black person. Even her movements were typically white, with that limp angularity in the joints, that quattrocento quality in her bearing, which is not found in suppler black bodies and in whites can degenerate into woodenness. Maria had the appearance not of a *mulatto*, but of a full-blooded black girl in whom certain features of an ancestor who was certainly not black had nonetheless asserted themselves. Even later, after he had begun his European travels, Ruprecht had felt the need to inquire about this girl from his childhood. Gradually the information he gleaned about her had coalesced into a coherent story, though subsequently he had not given it a thought for years. She was the child of the steward's eldest daughter. The mother had died in childbirth, and her father had paid little attention to her since.

The man was the type that can be described without hesitation as not 'careful'. His name was Theodoor and, like Frits, he had found his way to Europe. Frits had encountered him as a waiter in a classy

Hague restaurant, but also as the doorman of a Paris dive where Frits mostly went to see lesbians dancing together, with faces so pained they resembled drowning souls just retrieved from the water. That was the father, Theodoor. His daughter Maria, with the help of Ruprecht's parents, had been able to study at the college in the island's only town to become a teacher, third class. That entitled her, with her look of slight disbelief, to stand day in day out in front of a class of poor black children, while with arms neatly crossed they recited their monotonous tables: ab, bc, cd... three four five, one two three. That afternoon in town this chanting had wafted towards him, but at the time he paid it scarcely any attention. Perhaps it had been her conducting the chanting. He resolved at any rate to trace her before he boarded the boat and left this island again. Because for all the expectations of far-fetched adventures he knew he would not be staying long and that this short stay would be limited to discussions with the old notary. He took a few paces backwards, until his heels touched the threshold.

Pondering these matters, he had strolled outside. With the narrow threshold between heel and sole he rocked up and down. He felt a smile spreading over his face: he was far from happy but felt himself caught up in a mood of contentment. Before him lay the darkness, which he had peopled with tender images from childhood. Behind him he could hear the clatter of knives and forks in the dining room, and the sound of plates striking the table top. It was the housekeeper preparing dinner for him.

'How dark it is tonight. In Europe they think there are only clear moonlit and starlit nights in the tropics.'

The housekeeper did not answer.

'When does the moon rise?'

'There's no moon tonight,' she replied in a clear voice that almost tempted him to turn round and look at the woman who went with the voice. But he did not turn round. He wanted to stand like this for a little while; rocking up and down with the narrow threshold between heel and sole and, behind his back, the light of the hanging lamp, the clatter and thud of the cutlery and plates, the shuffling of the woman's sandals over the concrete.

The sense that the housekeeper was constantly moving around

him gave him a safe feeling, almost as if he were being caressed; she was like a cat, also scarcely glimpsed but constantly present. He was truly happy that he had not turned round; this was perfect: knowing she was there without having seen her. The housekeeper, a slim black woman, was bending under the hanging lamp which, because of the white tablecloth, appeared to be emitting a light several times more powerful; she carefully arranged something on the table. When she had finished, she picked up the empty tray, on which she had brought in plates and food, and walked slowly past the arcades back to the kitchen, where she placed the empty tray on a table. As she disappeared from the room she had sneaked a look at Frits Ruprecht, who was still standing with his back to her. In the kitchen she blew some more life into the fire in the stove, then sat down at a table and began massaging her forehead pensively with her fingers. She got up, lit a lantern and went outside. The wind flapped at her skirt, which was only just below knee length. She walked slowly down the terrace, then strolled round the terrace in the dark. The lantern swayed gently like an incense-burner. The light fell occasionally on a cactus stalk that loomed up out of the darkness and soared into the air. In the bushes the lizards started awake and fled rustling through the leaves. The light swung across the bare ground where even the humblest pebble cast its own deep shadow. Reaching a plot full of lush vegetation, she set down the lantern and squatted. Patches of light and dark alternated among the leaves and stalks. The woman's body too was only fragmentarily lit: her neck, her face and her legs. The occasional ray of light caught the toe of one sandal. She watched as a snail shell wobbled its way over some clods of earth. A caterpillar seated on a heart-shaped leaf was alarmed by the change in light level and half its body writhed in the air. A flower-head loomed up out of the darkness, cut free from its stalk, only the base of which was fully lit. The woman ran her hands through the leaves and tendrils of the melons, and tugged one of the melons loose, pressing her lips together in determination at the exertion.

Meanwhile Frits Ruprecht was sitting at table with a smile on his face – a contented, indifferent smile, now that munching food had brought him back to reality and to scepticism about the often convoluted stories with which people try to fool each other. He had been told that Maria was Theodoor's daughter. That might be so, or the truth might be totally different. He stopped eating and put down his knife and fork. With teeth clenched and eyes narrowed in a shrewd expression, he gave free rein to his own malicious musings. He came from this island too, he knew the score, he saw through the fictions. It would not surprise him if one fine day the actual father turned to be not the slovenly Theodoor but Alexander Ruprecht, Frits' father. He knew that men like Theodoor, destined to end up serving in European bars, were often chosen as a cover for the peccadilloes of white gentlemen. But there was one way in which these white sinners revealed themselves: they gave their secret children an education, thus making the children and themselves suspect in the eyes of others. What betrays people most remains their own heart and a small number of irresistible impulses... Frits turned his head. He had heard the scuffing of the sandals at the back of the house. He would have liked to talk to another human being, but she had already disappeared into the room on the right in the back section, where she probably slept. Frits smiled and repeated meaningfully, almost obscenely to himself: 'Where she probably *sleeps*.' Under his breath he went on, raising his index finger and threatening the imaginary person opposite him: 'Yes Daddy-o, Daddy-o, heavens knows what you got up to here. Perhaps all of us on the plantation are your children, Our Father who art in heaven.' Immediately afterwards his face darkened: it was as if the inappropriate remark and particularly the cheerful tone had issued from someone else. He continued his meal in cowed silence, castigated by his own child's conscience. Then he wiped his mouth and clenched the napkin in his fist. He got up. He took the briefcase, in which he had brought the bare essentials, off the chair next to him, and went into the room where he used to sleep, to the right of the living room, opposite the door he had shut when the glowing eyes bore down on him. He left the door open until he had found a paraffin lamp on a table with a brass dish as a reflector. He fiddled with the lamp, lit the wick and slid the glass back down. The room was windowless, but did have a second door that looked out onto the terrace. There was a kind of camp bed. He remembered how often in Europe he had longed to sleep in such a bed, especially because no blankets were used, only two very thin sheets. On the wall was a framed picture, which he also remembered from the past, of a very young girl, kneeling in her nightdress with hands clasped in prayer. Pre-Raphaelite. He had once come across the original in the Tate or the National Gallery. He had stood rooted to the spot, because it seemed like a copy of the picture on the distant plantation, just as the face he now examined carefully in the round mirror above the table seemed a dishevelled copy of his earlier child's face. He remembered the compulsory short haircut; his father considered hair of any length utterly disgusting. As a result the double crowns on his forehead twisted his hair into a pointed lock, a miniature Napoleonic curl, which he himself had always found ridiculous. Grimly he pulled open the drawer of the table. It was full of all kinds of shells. He remembered that his father, who generally took pleasure in very little, was occasionally entranced by the shells:

'Will you give your father this shell, Frits?'

He wondered if the shells he had given his father as gifts still existed. If so, they must be in one of the drawers of his father's desk. Frits was going to investigate immediately. He hurried out of the room. He had already opened the door, and was heading for the three-masted ship under full sail in a bottle, the typewriter under its shroud, the rifles and the revolvers. When his father was away it was from the study that he had occasionally climbed up to where the bats swayed like wisps of black cotton wool. The memory of the ghost-like creatures held no terrors for him now that, feeling as secure as the little boy who ran frenetically in one door and out the other, he roamed through his parents' house. The door handle, in which his hand recognised the old dents, felt familiar to the grip. He had already progressed some way through the living room, and was already turning towards the threshold to the front of the house, when he involuntarily stopped in his tracks.

In the furthest arch, in the direction of the kitchen he had seen Maria's face. The shock sent the blood coursing erratically through his veins. The tips of his fingers tingled, almost hurting. He stood there like a halfwit, both hands extended, with blank astonishment in his eyes and face.

Slowly the shock subsided, and he heard the ticking of the mahogany wall clock in the back of the house. Until then its sound had not registered with him this evening. The soothing peace of the living room, lit by the paraffin lamp, flowed into him. Odd how the look of things can change according to our state of mind. The same room, which at the start of the evening had alarmed him with its flower-head of light, into which he plunged as if into something incorporeal, now reassured him with its harmless rustic lighting. It had been so long since Ruprecht had stood in this calm light. He looked up at the paraffin lamp. As if for the first time he looked at the tiny flashes of light on the reservoir. Around the reservoir his eyes followed the metal rim that was attached by hooks to three chains by which the lamp hung from the ceiling above the table.

The tiny clips that pressed the burner closer to the lamp glass, actually moved him, because such a trivial detail from the past was suddenly vividly present. It seemed almost impossible that one could be pursued by obsessive images in this peaceful atmosphere. Had it been real or another hallucination? However peaceful the light in the living room appeared, perhaps the deep shadows in the arches of the arcades had helped conjure up the adorable image of Maria's face. Or rather, the way he imagined little Maria's face must have developed into adulthood. Framed by the arch it resembled the pious enlargement of the domestic photo of a woman who had died young. She was wearing a white linen blouse, tucked into a black skirt. It was a European profile; the hair too was fuller than is usually the case with black women... But it was not possible... He had also heard the shuffle of the housekeeper's sandals. Maria could not possibly be a housekeeper here. She was a teacher in town, with the priests and nuns who brought their faith and their religious education to the little black children of the island. Pure coincidence: the housekeeper had some similarity with Maria, which was not surprising, since she was actually quite probably related to Maria...

Nevertheless he walked quickly, almost at a trot, to the kitchen. As he passed the arcade, he saw his own shadow flapping at his shoulder like a black cloak. He found no one in the kitchen. The fire in the stove was already out, and in the half-light he saw a cat curled in a ball on the wicker seat of a chair.

He retraced his steps. First glowing eyes and now Maria's face. Where was this leading? Why was this woman hovering around him so invisibly? She had cleared the table while he had been daydreaming about the Tate Gallery in his bedroom. Why this flitting about like a ghost? In the study he opened one of the drawers of the desk. The drawer was empty, though one panel was covered in dried up patches of ink. In another drawer was a Browning revolver, next to a yellow wooden ruler and an electric torch that he switched on for a moment; he put the Browning and the torch on the table, and then pushed the drawer shut. In the next drawer there were only a few balls of paper on an opened pack of candles. Not until he came to the fourth drawer did he find the shells he had gathered for his father in the white sand by the sea. Frits turned the shells over and over in his hand; with his fingers he felt their spines, but he could no longer appreciate the multicoloured shells and the mother-of-pearl sheen he had once admired. He stared vaguely ahead of him, saw the face framed by the arcade; he had seen the eyes shift sideways for a moment, fearfully, as if Frits might do her harm. Had he ever done Maria harm? Again his thoughts centred on the young girl with whom he had once sat in the palm garden on the moss-covered stone bench. His heart dissolved in pity... He remembered how he had once taken Maria to task. He had seen her lips tremble, but she had immediately pressed them together, like a brave girl who does not want to cry... Before the first tear fell, he had kissed her, somewhere on the cheek...

Who knows how unhappy she had felt later... If a young black man became a teacher, it was obvious what was motivating him, what his ambitions were. He wanted to get on in the world, instead of remaining a servant. A girl like Maria, on the other hand, became a teacher because she wanted to live up to the demands made on her, no more than that... Who had imposed the demand of becoming a teacher? A girl like Maria would also be capable of returning to her origins, just as Frits had returned to his... So for all he knew she might well, acting on an inner urge, have traded in her job as a teacher at the girls' school for life on the plantation. Acting on an inner urge taking her back to her origins. She had discarded the stockings, and with them the high heels.

Frits was only fantasizing, with the shell in his hands. He finally dropped the shell back into the drawer, among the rest; he picked out another, to which he paid equally little attention. His fantasizing helped convince him that it really was Maria he had seen, and imperceptibly a strange exultation crept into the visions.

She had discarded the stockings and with them the high heels. There she stood again in her sandals, just as back then she had played with Frits at various places on the plantation: the beach, or the palm garden. Perhaps also in the garden that they had made together, just behind the house; there they sowed beans, melons, but also unknown seeds pilfered from drawers from which only time would tell what would grow. For all he knew, Maria had expanded this garden and still squatted there attentively by a stalk with two seed pods on it, or by the melon tendrils as fuzzy and hairy as insect legs. Perhaps she also grew those useless things called flowers: roses, dahlias, camellias... But who or what could have prompted her to abandon teaching and come back here to the plantation?

It probably happened like this. She probably fell ill in the arid, lifeless town. It was probably not only the high-heeled shoes that constrained her. No. The nuns and the father would have been sure to exert their dreadful pressure on her. She would have fallen ill and so spent a few weeks with her grandfather, the steward. Probably she went back, and returned sick a second time. And one day the thought took shape in her mind: quite simply not to go back, so she no longer had to wear high heels, no longer had to climb aboard the bus that passed twice a day, no longer had to endure audiences with Mother Superior... Just to stay here... Among the melons, the roses, the palms... The north-east trade wind blows through your hair... Life becomes sad, but full of a meaning that it lacks else-where. Frits Ruprecht smiled affectionately. To manage this she must surely have had to spin a yarn to the steward. He, with his eyes staring blindly into the distance, was probably surprised that a girl would want to give up her young lady's existence for that of a simple maid on a plantation...

Perhaps she had not spun the steward a yarn at all. Perhaps she had never returned to the plantation and these were just fantasies in Frits' brain. But he could not get out of his mind the other tantalising, almost frightening, possibility: that he was now just a few yards away from her, that he had only to push open a door to experience the softness of her presence. Frits felt an irresistible urge mounting in him to go to Maria's room, wake her, ask her how she had managed it, and whether his father had helped her. Whether she wanted to stay here for ever... and be without a man like this... and gradually dry up... and pine away like an autumn leaf sinking deeper in the earth and fading...

Frits put the shells back together, sweeping them back into a heap as he had found them. Slowly he began pushing the drawer shut. The drawer scarcely moved. Frits thought: why don't I go to her and comfort her, the woman who after all really is my black sister? It was a safe assumption that she actually was his sister, that she was the daughter not of Theodoor, who pushed revolving doors for drowning lesbians, but of Alexander Ruprecht, Frits' father, who one night had been enchanted by the steward's daughter, as unexpectedly as by the pink inside the shells.

Frits slammed the drawer shut and left the study. At the front of the house he noticed that the woman had once again flitted through the house, while he had been thinking about Maria in the study: she had blown out the lights at the front and back of the house and only in the living room was the light still on, turned down low. A woman was hovering around him in smaller and smaller circles, or was it he who was moving around the woman and approaching her?

As he moved towards her room, a last doubt assailed him: was she Maria and was Maria really his sister? But then he forgot all doubts, no longer listening to the voice of reason, and found himself in a different world. He had already reached the door of her room. He opened it, took one step and then another into her room, but held onto the door knob behind him, and did not close the door. In the dark he heard how quietly she lay there, scarcely breathing. A strange *volte-face* had occurred in his feelings for Maria. He heard the rush of the silence, heard the rush of his own blood. The scent of the woman hung in the room. He felt as if he were moving towards something new, brilliant. It was no longer the child in Maria that moved him, but the woman who intoxicated him beyond measure... Maria, or that other woman who resembled her and who tonight could not be anyone but Maria... It struck him how strangely they had been thrown together tonight... Here,

where everything was so far from Asia, America, and Europe with
their gloomy aspirations, which, he seemed to remember, he
himself had shared for a while... How insignificant their two help-
less bodies seemed to him, breathing slowly – like livestock in the
corral – in this white house on the hill, every glimmer of which had
been engulfed by the night and every sound by the rustle of palms
and sea. It was not only this mellowing solitude that drove him
towards her. In his active imagination he saw his fragile little sister
grow into a young woman. He stood and watched, entranced. And
this rapturous contemplation of the ripening of the familiar girl's
body awakened in him the desire for her female completion, for her
embraces, for her womanly curves. His hand was still resting on the
doorknob. He could still hear her lying there silently, scarcely
breathing. With his heart in his mouth he closed the door. It was so
dark that he could not see his hand in front of his face...

Maria, or the other woman, did not resist him; she abandoned
even her timid attempts. The arms that she threw round his neck,
bound him convulsively to her for a moment. She released him and
holding him at arm's length, said, 'Do you know, Frits, how I've
always remembered you? As the little boy, apart from the others,
with your double crown, your curl, your mean mouth...'

For a moment he was startled by the inexorable fact that it really
was Maria. But with a laugh she enfolded him in her arms: mean
little Frits. His body relaxed in her embrace until it was he who was
embracing and it was her body that relaxed. His hand was already
caressing the curve of her hip, the emotion of his heart was already
overflowing into bodily desire, when the sound of violent rattling at
the front door penetrated the room. Frits immediately jumped up
and stood next to the bed. Tears of rage welled up in his eyes, and he
could taste the bitterness in his mouth. He barked a question at her:

'Have you got a guy somewhere around?'

'A guy, Frits?'

'Don't play games. Have you got a guy? Yes or no?'

'No. But what is it, Frits? Let me go and open up.'

'No. You're staying here.'

They wouldn't catch him out. You couldn't fool Frits Ruprecht
as easily as that. He locked the door of her room, but could still

hear her voice: 'Frits, why are you doing that?'

In the living room he blew out the lamp, so that the house was in darkness. He went to his father's study, grabbed the Browning, pulled out the magazine: it was empty. He pulled out the drawers two at a time: no bullets to be found. He did, though, find cartridges for the hunting rifle standing in the corner. He slung the Browning and its holster across the table. He took hold of the hunting rifle, loaded it. He stuffed the remaining cartridges and the pocket torch into his pockets. He closed the door, so that no light could penetrate the house from here. He walked through the dark front section of the house to the front door. Again someone rattled at it. The sound drove him wild. When he reached the door he stopped, held his breath and listened. The moment the rattling began again, he wrenched at the door, which opened inwards. He immediately shone the torch at the visitor and saw the eyes of the steward staring blindly into the distance.

'What do you want at this hour, Wantsho? I thought you all went to bed at eight o'clock every night. That's the third time today you've upset me. Can't it wait till tomorrow?'

'Mr Frits...'

'Mr Frits nothing. Get going and off to bed with you. We can continue this tomorrow...'

'Mr Frits...'

'I remember that from long ago. Catching people by surprise in the middle of the night and thinking you'll get your way...'

'I don't want anything, Mr Frits...'

'We know all about that, not wanting anything. A goat for Auntie Carolina's party. Or a rabbit for Auntie Esmeralda's do. You can have it all. All right. But tomorrow. Not tonight. And off to bed, Wantsho. I don't want any more rattling. Good night.'

Just as he was about to slam the door in Wantsho's face, he heard screaming that was as unreal as just now when he opened the door of his mother's bedroom:

'Maria is your father's daughter!!'

He wrenched the door open again. He had no idea exactly what happened next. Probably he slipped on the worn threshold, fell and thrashed about with his arms so that the barrel of the rifle hit

Wantsho in the chest. When he had recovered and was back on his feet, his first thought was: 'Just as well it didn't fire.' That was all he needed. He helped old Wantsho, who had been knocked over by the blow and was groaning faintly, to his feet.

It was so dark that he had to grope his way. Nor could he see any stars: the sky was heavily overcast. In the blackness Frits Ruprecht could easily use words to hide his emotion from the other man, who had not yet recovered from the shock and whose teeth were chattering audibly.

'Nothing's happened, Wantsho. I just slipped and hit you in the chest with the rifle. It was your chest, wasn't it?'

'Yes, my chest…' Wantsho could scarcely get the words out.

'Shall we fetch some light and see what's wrong?'

'No, I won't come inside. It's better if Maria doesn't know about any of this. I've just had a shock, I'm not in pain.'

'All right, Wantsho. Let me just take you back till you've got over the shock.'

Wantsho allowed himself to be led by the arm, while Ruprecht reassured him.

'I just slipped. You mustn't worry about it. You should know that I myself had a faint suspicion that Theodoor was only being used as a cover. A perfectly natural suspicion, since my father had paid for Maria to qualify as a teacher. I've no need to hide anything from you. You're an old man, your life was worth more to my father than mine, so you've a right to know everything.'

The gravel of the drive crunched under their feet. A glow worm lit up and then faded, the only illumination in the dark night. The way the old man rested on his arm convinced Ruprecht that he needed to accompany him a little further.

'I admit that your granddaughter is a beautiful girl, Wantsho. "I am black, but comely, O ye daughters of Jerusalem." Do you remember that, from the Song of Solomon? I suspect you know the Bible better than I do. If I had had absolutely no inkling of this, there might have been something to fear. But Wantsho, dear Wantsho, why were you in such a hurry?'

Ruprecht felt the arm he was supporting gradually beginning to free itself.

'Wantsho, I think you take me for more wicked than I am.'

He heard Wantsho shuffling along beside him. He could have gone on walking for hours next to the old man like this, silent and without a thought in his head. But the last thing he wanted to do was to be a nuisance; the moment he realised that the other man no longer needed support, he took his leave.

'Well, Wantsho. Let's shake hands. Goodnight.'

'Goodnight, Mr Frits. I'm sorry. I've seen many accidents. Including some I could have protected others from.'

For a moment the frail old black hand rested in the young white hand.

'Goodnight, Wantsho.'

The two of them parted. Wantsho walked on. Ruprecht stared in the direction in which he disappeared until he could no longer hear the footsteps.

He stood in the silence unable to make up his mind, but then jerked round. He had heard rustling behind his back. He listened. It sounded like human whispers. For a moment he thought he heard the plod of footsteps and giggling laughter. He was alert, on his guard; it was so like the whispering and laughing of human beings. But it must be the wind gusting in the palm leaves, springing back, creaking and rasping. For some reason it reminded him of Karel, who found it impossible to laugh without gloating. But Karel was sitting at home reading *Othello*, with his unfathomable smile midway between resolve and hostility. This rather unpleasant memory of Karel, however, glided past him as fast as the breeze that blew through his hair... Frits turned round. A hard slog back to the house, where he had found a sister, but lost a lover. He was so tired that he gave only a moment's thought to possible excuses he might make to Maria, before immediately abandoning the attempt. What would be, would be! But when he unlocked her door and found the light on in her room, he realised that Wantsho's anxious cry had penetrated here too. She was lying half upright on the bed, eyes wide open, looking at the ground. He sat down next to her, not knowing what to say, and looked at the ground too. Finally he put his arm round her shoulder. He pressed his face against hers. She did not stop him but her face did not return the pressure like his mother's used to. They sat there side by side for a moment. Then he began rocking her slowly back and forth. At the same time, as he had done with his mother, he produced the humming sound from deep in his chest, without parting his teeth. The tears rolled slowly from her eyes...

Life became sad, but full of a meaning that it lacks elsewhere. And that is the only thing no one can take away from the children of this earth.

The Swimmer: A Holiday Story

Anna Blaman

translated by Paul Vincent

It wasn't deliberate, we hadn't arranged it, it's just how things turned out. She leading the way, I right behind her, we stumbled across the jagged rocky shore and the deserted shingle beaches till there was no one else to be seen. A thoroughly exhausting trek, partly because the sea made such a din we had to shout to make ourselves understood. It was blowing a gale and there was no sun at all, and I was kicking myself for not having just stayed in the village; what was there for us to do here, except discover that it was even more miserable than back there? But then we stopped, both panting like refugees, and as I looked around me, disgruntled and close to collapse, first out to sea and then at the rocky land, I heard her say, 'Let's lie here, it'll be quiet here'. And she stretched out on the narrow shingle beach and looked up. 'Here,' she said again, 'here you can forget that anyone else exists apart from you and me, here you're right on the borderline between the world and the sea, in a kind of no-man's-land. Just stop thinking about anything. Listen to the sea and look into the universe, there's nothing more therapeutic.' I hadn't joined her, I just sat there, stubbornly, upright, as if at any minute I might jump up again and continue on my way. I said, 'Therapeutic! That was what you said, wasn't it?' The waves roared towards us and the universe was shut tight. But when I glanced sideways at her face I saw she was laughing, certain that she was wiser than I was. So why didn't I lie down, among the low rocks, out of the wind, in a spot so lonely that human preoccupations seemed a lifetime away? Why didn't I do that, for my own good? In such a lonely spot, were there really just the two of us here? I glanced furtively around me on the beach and immediately discovered that there was someone else, perhaps a hundred metres further on. I couldn't have spotted him earlier, though, as he must have undressed behind one of the jagged rocks and now I watched him head for the water for a swim. 'There's someone else,' I said. She didn't move, but kept gazing up with a lazy, peaceful smile. 'I wouldn't look, if I were you.' And then: 'I wouldn't be able to look anyway, I'm lying here like a stone among the other stones on the beach, like a speck of dust on the bottom of the universe.' And without even looking at me she groped blindly for my hand and said, 'Just do as I do, it's wonderful, doing nothing, thinking nothing, just being...' And still clutching my hand: 'So there's nothing that can hurt me any more and nothing to strive for... except: to be one with the stones, a speck of dust in the universe.' But though it sounded like a commandment, a liberating magic formula from the secret of nature that surrounded us, it had no effect on me. I remained who and what I was, I remained my utterly lonely self and looked desolately across the beach and the sea. I saw how the swimmer had now virtually reached the water. He walked very cautiously, obviously finding the rocks and pebbles painful, and stopped indecisively. The water was of course icy and on top of that there was a powerful undertow when the waves retreated. Listen to how many pebbles are dragged along, with a crunching sound, whole lorryloads at a time! It was actually crazy to go swimming now. 'You can't do it,' I heard next to me, 'you sit there and look. As long as there is a single person to be seen, you can't rest.' She stroked my hand. 'I'd be inclined to think you were crazy about people.' 'Oh, I'm not so sure about that,' I said. 'This morning, for instance,' she went on, 'in that shop and then in that restaurant, I thought something similar.' 'Oh did you? And why then?' 'Oh, you know very well,' she said and then kept her hand still on mine. Of course we had exchanged a look of understanding, first over that woman behind the counter who got everything wrong, weighing, adding up the bill, because she was oh so frightened of that husband of hers who, with icy hilarity and petty hatred, sat and watched how badly she ran the shop... and then over that child in the restaurant that obeyed his mother's orders as if his life depended on it, and oh that piercing French voice and that panicky obedience like that of a dog frightened of the whip! But OK, a look of understanding, what does it mean? Definitely not that you understand each other. And she, next to me, is so different from me, we're complete opposites; if she has to she can even laugh where anyone else would cry. 'But you,' she says suddenly, 'time and time again you're the victim of your imagination, you immediately see a whole life behind an insignificant incident like that; you see the grocer's wife and that child in the concentration camp of lovelessness, you see them spiritually starving, being tormented, driven to madness and finally dying like beasts.' I looked out over the sea. 'No,' I said without taking my eyes off the sea, 'no, it's not like that, a melodramatic story, however true it might be, I didn't fantasise on top of it at any rate. But what it is like, is difficult to say...' Meanwhile I saw the swimmer fighting the surf, determined, efficient; he dived right under high oncoming waves, swam three or four strokes and then dived again. It was a beautiful contest of cunning against brute force. Soon he would be through the dangerous surf and in an area that scarcely deserved the name of sea; it was more reminiscent of a huge turmoil of mighty reptiles, poisonous green with foam-topped waves... And meanwhile I felt the woman next to me beginning to stroke my hand again and heard her say, 'Am I wrong then? So what was going on in you?' I pulled my hand free, since she might have to laugh, which is also why I did not look at her when I said, 'What concerned me was more the attitude of the two others than the fate of their victims... I don't know if you understand me.' She laughed, out loud. 'Of course, Anna, go ahead and say it! Don't be frightened of a word that the whole world bandies about. Love! There should be a bit more love! Then the grocer's wife would instantly feel safe and weigh and tot up with the best of them, and the boy would no longer live in his concentration camp but would play on the beach with other boys like a normal, happy-go-lucky boy!' And again she laughed, not maliciously but confidently, amused, because she had again proved how well she knew me, better than I knew myself if I were to believe her. I turned towards her and snapped, 'You take me for an idiot, but you're wrong again. I'm not talking about love, you won't catch me doing that. I'm just thinking of a reasonable amount of attention, not out of love for each other (that's asking too much, much too much), but just to make life possible for each other to live. Listen,' – I changed tone, because I now felt I could really say what I meant – 'a little attention for each other, by way of human decency, cultivated as a habit, that's all, how do think the world would look then?' – I gave her a compelling look, and I could see very well that she was having diffi-culty in not bursting out laughing and only just managing to control herself. After all, she was fond of me. And so she touched my face with a caressing hand, and said with a trembling voice, trembling with suppressed laughter, 'Oh, the world would be a paradise. Not a soul would ever feel they had been thrown to the wolves, not a soul could ever be lost.' – But then she quickly pulled my face towards her, pressed her cheek against mine and whispered, 'But do you know it could never, never happen? How unhappy and arrogant you are! What on earth do you imagine? Wouldn't that mean dividing up the "God sees us" among people... So it would become "We see each other". Just imagine!' And then it really became too much for her and she burst out laughing. I had one more try, and said, 'And why not? Isn't that what man is eventually supposed to inherit spir-itually?' But she went on laughing, without malice certainly, more affectionately, but still I could not stand it any longer – after all we were talking about one of my loftiest notions. And I got up and the moment I was standing upright the wind leaped upon me as if it had been lying in wait and I felt immediately in the midst of a howling storm. I braced myself and began walking, with her behind me, calling 'Anna, crazy, darling Anna, you're not angry, are you?' – I shook my head. No, I wasn't, but then why did she go on laughing, was I ridiculous perhaps? 'Of course not, but you know what it is, my dear Anna, I'm too cynical and you're too good, believe me, that's what it is… ' And so I walked along the beach, and the mounting waves charged malevolently towards it, and behind them, the sea again lay like a tangle of hissing reptiles, and I walked on for about a hundred metres and then suddenly stopped and the woman following me did likewise. At my feet lay the swimmer's clothes. And even before I started scanning the sea, that deserted water desert in the storm, I knew. He was nowhere to be seen. He had long since ceased swimming, he had long since started drifting deep below the howling surface in a silence we called absolute or eternal.

But the woman next to me did not raise her eyes. She stood motionless, as if mesmerised, and just looked, as if mesmerised, at that wretched heap of clothes… until I said, 'We've got to report it right away.' Only then did she start moving again, but without looking at me. She must feel deep sympathy for me to blot out my devastation so neatly. And so she of course remained outside when I went to report that I had seen a man swimming, but that the exact moment at which he must have drowned had escaped my attention.

In Praise Of Navigation

Gerard Reve

translated by Paul Vincent

Four years ago, at the end of winter, I began preparing for my first expedition to England. I had studied both the *King James Bible* and the Watchtower Bible & Tract Society version, and in addition had acquainted myself with *The American Language* by HL Mencken, *Sexual Behavior in the Human Male* by Kinsey, Pomeroy and Martin, *The Golden Bough* by Sir James Frazer and *The Varieties of Religious Experience* by William James. Those with a purpose let nothing deter them. However, it had become clear to me that direct contact with the spoken language was needed. I had already spread out an old pink flannel blanket on the floor in one corner, on which could be placed, in the weeks preceding departure, objects or goods to be taken, as and when they occurred to me, such as matches, darning wool, razor blades, bars of soap, lighter fuel and flints, all of which are more expensive abroad. I had virtually no money and was looking for ways to make the crossing for nothing or very cheaply.

To this end I resolved to send a well-argued request to a number of shipping companies to provide me with a free or greatly reduced passage. I still have the copies, which I occasionally find among other papers, and am mortified. I already possessed a measure of *savoir faire*. Céline's testimony, for example, that the truth must be concealed at all costs and the moment one has attracted the attention of the authorities one must make oneself scarce as soon as possible, had made a deep impression on me. But I did not yet know that one must never ever disclose the fact that one is a writer. I was already gloomy and melancholy, and already knew that I had wasted a large part of my life, which had consisted of little but misery, and that if God granted me time, much more wretchedness awaited me, but I had still retained many generous, optimistic notions, for instance that people really were interested in others, that things obvious to me could therefore also be made clear to others, that there was perceptible progress in human society, and that ordinary people were interested in literature.

So I wrote the letters, explaining my difficulties, and received a reply from only one company in the form of a standard business postcard folded in half and secured with staples, informing me that my request could unfortunately not be granted. Still, I persisted in my efforts. An acquaintance who occupied a responsible position in an export company was able to use that position to pressure a freight company, which shipped a great deal for his firm, to take me from Amsterdam to London. To simplify things, he made me a student. He informed me of his success and told me where I was to report at the time of departure. It turned out to be the same company that had sent the solitary, negative, response to my letter. My acquaintance in the export company had not given my name, so that I was now afraid that if it now became known all the effort might even now prove to be in vain.

One Saturday afternoon in March, in wet, stormy weather, after a tram ride to a part of town where I had never been before, I presented myself at an office building on one of the quays in Amsterdam harbour. In the distance, at the end of the quay, low in the water, lay a small vessel with many cargo booms, which I took for a canal boat. I went into the office, where it turned out that no one knew a thing about me. However, besides the name of the shipping company, I also knew that of one of its executives, which I mentioned, mumbling that he must know about it. The person in question was evidently known, but he was thought not to be in.

There was a conference at a reception window. I had been given two o'clock as the ship's time of departure, and an ugly round wall clock in the office pointed to this time. A ship's siren that sounded close by brought me close to panic.

At the window it was decided that the person I mentioned might be somewhere further along the quay. I left the office and went in the direction indicated as far as a customs checkpoint. Here I asked to be let through provisionally, left my kitbag behind and reached the boat I had seen from a distance. It was an extraordinarily small craft, with its middle deck scarcely out of the water, and was in the process of being loaded. There was no sign of any other ship, so this must be the vessel about to depart.

I asked the man on the quay, who seemed to be overseeing operations, about the person I was looking for. This turned out to be himself, but he too maintained that he knew nothing about a passage for me. The rain had got heavier and there were such violent gusts of wind that snatches of the conversation were carried away and had to be repeated.

The man surveyed me impatiently and with his hand wiped a quantity of water, which threatened to run into the collar of his oilskin, out of his ginger hair and his blotchy, coarse face. 'I'll hear all about it in a bit,' he said. 'Go ahead and get on board.' I informed him that my bag of luggage was still at customs. 'I'll fetch it,' he declared. I had no alternative but to go up the gangplank. The forward part of the ship was being loaded with timber. I stopped somewhere amidships. A tall man with a yellow face and dirty-coloured hair was suddenly close to me, jumped nimbly over something and landed next to me. 'It's that way,' he said, pointing to a door. 'But the old man probably won't be there yet. Still in church, I reckon.' He contorted his face into a grin, revealing a row of bad teeth, and suddenly let out a deep moan, put his hand on his stomach and with half-closed eyes rocked his head back and forth, while the moaning turned to a faint hum. 'Boy, oh boy,' he murmured.

I thanked him, went to the door he had indicated, knocked, received no answer, hesitated and then went in. I found myself in the captain's lounge. I sat down at the table, dried myself off with my handkerchief, and waited. The room made a gloomy impression.

On the wall hung a barometer in a miniature steering wheel, as well as a pendulum clock with a pine cone weight. On an imitation mantelpiece there were photos of two extremely ugly, unhealthy-looking children, a boy and a girl. On a stained bookshelf empty of books, in the groove of a plaster base, was a round frosted glass plate with an electric bulb behind it and in front a plaster shepherdess with two dogs. A substance had seeped out from beneath the base and set hard, from which I concluded that the base had been glued down to counteract the movement of the ship. On a fairly wide window-sill there were small objects made of new copper, including a jug, a barrel and a match holder. There was a brown plush sofa with women's magazines lying in one corner. There were also a granite draining board and a sink in a corner of the room, both fringed with pelmets of pink check material.

From somewhere down below slow footsteps ascended, in the direction of the two doors opposite me. The right-hand door was opened and I stood up. A slim woman of between thirty-five and forty came in. I said hello and introduced myself. After a moment's hesitation, she took my hand awkwardly, as if she were not used to shaking hands, and immediately let go of it again. 'Are *you* travelling with us?' she asked reproachfully. 'I thought two ladies were coming.' She had a Northern accent. She was wearing a badly-fitting brown dress, with cloth buttons that closed up to the throat. Her dark blond hair, which was dull and seemed to have been bleached by washing with inferior soaps, was wound around a plastic roller at the back. Across the skin of her dour, bespectacled face lay that particular patina of greyness that one finds so often in women from the provinces. She did not sit down, but fussed around at the sink and in a cupboard beneath it.

'I suppose you're a student?' she asked.

'Yes, well, actually yes, yes, I'm still studying,' I said. I prepared for a fuller explanation of this rather incomplete answer, but the woman said nothing and stood at one of the windows. The rain was driven in occasional gushes against the glass by the howling wind.

'Dreadful weather, isn't it,' I observed. The woman did not react. She stood where she was and looked past the window pane at a corner of the room. I avoided looking at her and told myself she was busy doing something or other, although it was obvious that she wasn't doing anything.

'Are you a friend of Rev Kwakel's?' she asked, breaking the silence. I pulled a face as if thinking hard.

'Rev Kwakel,' I repeated softly. 'No, I don't know him.' That brought the conversation to a final halt. If I had been at home on the ship, I might have said I was just going to see how this or that was getting on, or that I was just going for a breath of fresh air. As it was I could not do the first, while in addition walking on deck in this weather would have been odd to say the least. I started sweating and a good deal of my courage began to fail me. I was worried about my luggage, which was still at customs, about my name that might still, at the last moment, put them on the trail of the previous correspondence, about the two ladies who would probably come and demand my place, and about the very general question whether, in the general sense I had any right to be in this parlour. I was in a situation in which the best thing to do is stare at the floor and speak nonsense words and sentences to oneself. So that was what I did. 'Blue dooby-doo, pom-pom,' I said to myself. Can't do a thing, a thing, tom, pom deeom. God our Saviour. Pitfalls, all pitfalls. The howling owl, hoop, hoop. A mess. Reedeboo, hop.'

The woman sat down and seemed to be looking for something in a drawer.

The captain and a smartly dressed elderly man now crossed the deck towards the room. As they came in I saw, to my considerable relief, that the captain was carrying my kitbag. He seemed to be in his mid-thirties, was sturdily built, his hair was already thinning, and he had the usual, slightly too fleshy mariner's face. His features were somewhat dour, but not exactly malevolent. In his eyes, however, there was an expression of obvious bitterness and distrust. I introduced myself to both of them. The smartly dressed gentleman sat down and carefully took my name in the corner of a sheet of paper. His left eye looked completely sideways the whole time.

'You're aware of the terms?' he asked sternly.

'Ten guilders, I believe,' I replied, since this was what I had been told.

'Five guilders a day,' shouted the man, waving the sheet to dry it, 'with a minimum of ten guilders. I'll bring you a note shortly.' Again I had visions of the correspondence being discovered. The man got up, put the sheet in his pocket and left.

'You might as well take that below,' said the captain, pointing to my kitbag. I picked it up and he pointed to the left hand of the two doors. Behind it a companion-way led to a cabin with two bunks one on top of the other. Should I not stay here for the time being? I wondered. In fact the lounge served as a living room for the captain and his wife, so what right did I have to sit there? I started unpacking some toilet things, occasionally looking out of one of the portholes, and then sat there without doing anything. I decide not to show myself again until I was asked. In this way I hoped to find out where I was expected to spend my time during the day.

After about ten minutes I was called. The smartly dressed gentleman got me to sign a typed declaration, releasing the shipping company from all liability, and then disappeared for good.

'The gentleman's a student,' said the woman.

'Would you like a cigarette?' asked the captain pointing to a glass box on the table. I helped myself and sat down in the first available seat. The captain put down some papers, leafed through them and signed them. Then he looked outside, across the deck, where loading had been completed and the canvasses had been secured over the timber, pulled open the door of a cabinet and turned on a radio. He searched the airwaves, passing both Hilversum stations, looked at his watch, pressed for a different wavelength and went on looking.

'It's on the world service, isn't it?' said the woman.

'Yes, that's what I'm trying to find.' He stopped the dial at a Dutch-language station. '... and in particular the sick, and those in pain', said a voice. 'We pray You, grant them faith and strength, so that they may find You and cling to You and receive solace from You. Amen.' A small choir launched into a psalm. The captain remained sitting sideways on to the radio. His wife, who had sat down at the table, stared at one of the windows that had misted over with the increased condensation. Her thin mouth had tightened even further. Neither of them moved until the singing had finished.

'Are they playing again back there?' asked the woman, cocking her head to one side as if listening to distant sounds.

'No, no way,' replied the captain. 'Are you Catholic by any chance?' he suddenly asked me.

'No, no, not at all,' I replied.

'Well, you could easily have been,' he said severely. I nodded. Another silence ensued. The captain closed the radio cabinet and went ashore. I strolled down to my cabin and stayed there for a considerable time without doing anything. Then a variety of different sounds combined to give me the impression that the ship was putting to sea, and I stumbled back up, so as to go outside via the lounge. However, the captain's wife was in the room. A paraffin stove was burning on the draining board. 'Would you like some tea?' she asked. I accepted her invitation and sat down.

'How long are you going to London for?' she asked.

'For two or three months,' I told her.

'What are you studying?' she asked, after she had filled my cup.

I took a deep breath and informed her that there had been a misunderstanding. I wasn't a student, but a writer. As I said this, for reasons I have never fully understood, my face began, as usual, to burn with embarrassment.

The woman observed me closely. The ship had begun to vibrate and gradually moved from the shore. She was probably about to say something when her man came in. 'I don't think we'll make it today,' he said.

'The gentleman isn't a student,' said the woman. 'The gentleman is a writer, he says.'

The captain looked at me, drawing the corners of his mouth downwards, and then stared at the table, but did not say anything. His wife asked if he wanted tea.

'I'd like to read first,' he replied. 'Yes,' she said softly and nodded.

The captain opened the cabinet again and took out a black book with no title on its spine that stood next to the radio, sat down, laid the book on the table and opened it where a woven leather bookmark lay between the pages. His wife also sat down. Inclining his head further forward and following the lines with his forefinger, he read:

Thus shalt thou also speak to Shemaiah the Nehelamite, saying thus speaketh the Lord of hosts, the God of Israel, saying because thou hast sent letters in thy name unto all the people that are at

Jerusalem, and to Zephaniah the son of Maaseiah the priest, and to all the priests, saying, the Lord hath made thee priest in the stead of Jehoida the priest, that ye should be officers in the house of the Lord, for every man that is mad, and maketh himself a prophet, that thou shouldest put him in prison and in the stocks...

For a moment I thought he had chosen the text for this occasion, but then realised that the bookmark had indicated the place. On deck a loud clumping of boots came very close to the door of the lounge. There was a knock.

'No, you bastard, watch it,' said a piercing voice that quickly trailed off into a whisper. The boots retreated again.

The captain read to the end of the chapter, closed the book, laid his hand on the binding, and closed his eyes. His wife also prepared herself for prayer. Once they had opened their eyes again, and the woman had given her husband tea, she asked, 'What kind of books do you write?'

'Novels... a novel... stories...' I mumbled. It seemed to me to be one big lie.

'Was that a novel, that book we borrowed from Luurd the other day?' asked the woman.

'What?' asked the captain in an irritated tone.

'I can't remember what it was called,' his wife assured him. 'This young chap first leaves his village. Then he goes to Paris, and to France, and so on, and then he joins the French Foreign legion. He keeps trying to leave the whole time, he wants to go back. He's wounded twice. Then he runs away again and goes back, but he's badly wounded. His stomach is shot to pieces. He's terribly wounded. But still he goes back home, and when he sees the girl again he dies. He dies in her arms. Henk is his name. It's all described. It's awful reading it, but you can't put it down. The writer has pictured it all. What was it called again?'

The captain shrugged his shoulders and stared angrily ahead of him.

'You wonder why anyone writes a book with such terrible things in it,' she said in conclusion.

'Do you write books like that?' asked the captain. 'Do you write dramatic books?'

'Well, that's not so easy to say,' I replied, looking round helplessly a few times and then staring straight ahead again. 'Dramatic, no...' I mumbled barely audibly. Again I had the sense that nothing I said was true, that I was lying and deceiving, and that under completely false pretences, like a parasite, I had found a passage on a ship with responsible, hard-working people. 'Bastard,' I said to myself.

'Have you written many books?' asked the woman, already with what I felt was considerable suspicion in her voice.

'Well... yes... I'll show you them...' I said, got up and went below. 'You're not a writer at all,' said a voice inside me. 'Show-off. Shit. Lord Muck.' I broke out in a sweat as I tugged the books out of my kitbag, and my whole body was on fire. 'How can you be so stupid, so stupid. It's no good. Oh, Christ,' the voice inside repeated. I trudged back up. Both of them carefully examined the covers and the title pages, and then put the volumes back on the table. There was another knock at the outside door. I picked up the books and disappeared, not too hurriedly, but as quickly as possible, back down below. I closed the cabin door, stowed the books at the bottom of the bag, and sat down on a chair. The green banks of the canal slid past the portholes. The grass waved wildly in the roaring wind. I peered at the brown-painted wood of the panelling, considered turning on the ceiling light so I could read, but sat there motionless. Many more questions remained. I had shown them the books, but might I not actually be someone completely different from the author? Why was I going to England, if it was not to study at an educational institution or do a job? What kind of person was I really, if people were to inquire about my family circumstances? I remembered that I had always envied people who were able to say in a couple of lines who and what they were: age, occupation, marital status, parents' occupation. I'm nothing at all, I thought, not even a con man. I decided to keep my head down for as long as possible. I lay down in the top bunk and tried to sleep. Instead the usual storm of useless thoughts blew up, a whirlwind of memories torn to shreds, like so many spirits screaming for vengeance in the night wind, without one knowing what they actually want. 'Bugger off,' I said aloud, but the images kept looming up, inexorably. I was reminded of how, twenty-two years ago, at the end of Ploegstraat, I had heard a woman say to another woman in the doorway of her flat, 'Lots of veg and not enough potatoes is no meal for a man.' Or the man who, in the starvation winter of 1944, as I was dragging away a felled tree early one morning, followed me in his shirtsleeves, screeching all the while, and tried to stand on the crown, which was still in leaf, repeating endlessly at the top of his voice, 'Those trees make oxygen!' Faces appeared, freeing themselves from the depths, some unfortunately of people who where still alive, but most, thank God, of those who were dead, their mouths contorted in angry reproach. 'Lord, Almighty, King of the Waters,' I thought. 'Take this vessel I beseech you. Swallow it up with all the living and writhing souls upon it.'

'How do I get anything to eat?' I began wondering, secretly eating an orange, wrapping the remains in paper and hiding them in my kitbag, I sat there on the edge of the bunk and let time drift by. It seemed to be getting darker. After spending a long time in a sort of stupor, I got up. I couldn't hear a sound in the lounge. I went in. There was no one there. Something was bubbling in a pan on the paraffin stove. I went on deck. It was only drizzling, but there was a north-west wind humming through the mast cables, so that you were wet through in an instant. In the wheelhouse I could see a number of figures behind the streaming glass. I shuffled about the deck for a bit and, keeping out of the wind as far as possible, made my way astern.

'Oy, George,' said a voice next to me suddenly. It was the man with the yellowish face who had shown me the way when I came on board. It was hanging out of the open top half of a hatchway. 'Want some tea?' he asked.

'I've had some,' I replied, stopping.

'Well, well,' said the figure in the hatchway. 'From her?' he then asked, pulling a funny face and nodding towards the lounge.

'From the captain's wife, yes,' I replied. The question might well be a ruse to expose my evil nature and ingratitude.

'I expect he told her to make you some,' he said.

'He didn't mention tea,' I said. 'He didn't want tea. He wanted to pray first.'

The cook or steward – that was what he must be, since while he was talking he busied himself with saucepans on a stove – sniggered.

'You'll see a thing or two,' he declared. 'The old man's not so bad. But that cow drives everyone nuts. Him too.'

I said nothing, but assumed an expression indicating that I was listening.

'We'll see who's driven nuts first,' he continued grimly, 'her or us.' He turned his attention to a kettle on the stove for a moment. 'She wants an organ on board,' he went on. 'We'll see about that.'

Ahead of me I could see a row of dunes looming up through the shrouds of rain. We were approaching IJmuiden.

'But surely the organ would go in the lounge?' I asked. 'It wouldn't disturb anyone else on the ship?' Behind us we heard two people coming down the steps from the bridge. 'Yes, take her over to starboard. Put her on the mud,' said a voice that was not the captain's.

The cook filled four cups with tea from a green enamel jug, whose contents I had the distinct impression had boiled, and put them on a plate.

'You can't hear a thing here, that's true,' he said with a leer. 'You'll have time to get to know her. We'll not be putting to sea today.'

'We're not crossing?' I asked.

'We'd lose all the timber,' he replied. 'Maybe tomorrow morning.' He came out carrying the plate with the cups on. 'Come with me,' he said. I followed him to the stern. We reached an area completely below deck consisting of a kind of mess room off which there were two cabins. The doors were open and in one cabin I saw a chaotic pile of clothes, washing, bedding and kitbags, with an accordion among them.

At a trestle table in the mess room itself sat two men of about thirty who looked as if they had just woken up: their hair was dishevelled, chins covered in stubble, and wearing only vests. I said hello and sat down at the table.

'You're a student, I suppose,' said the one sitting nearest. I hesitated, but then nodded.

'A cousin of mine's at teacher training college,' he announced. 'Study, study! Nothing but study!'

'Where's Berend got to?' asked the cook. The other two drank their tea, and the cook had taken the third cup, leaving only one on the tray.

'He'll be here any minute,' said the man who had talked about his cousin.

'And what about the student? Where's his tea then?' the other man asked. He was a little hoarse.

'He doesn't want any,' said the cook. He started rolling a cigarette.

'D'you know what I thought?' the hoarse man said to me. 'Actually I thought you were more like a painter or something. There's something artistic about him, dammit, that's what I thought.'

'Painter of nudes, you mean,' said the cook. 'What are you studying?'

'English,' I replied. I took out my tin of shag and offered it to the other two. They started rolling up.

The engines, which had been running more quietly for the last few minutes, now stopped completely. A slight shudder went through the ship for a moment, followed by a whooshing sound like a sigh. The ship listed slightly to port. Then there was silence. The ship, still listing to port, lay motionless.

'End of the line. All change,' shouted the hoarse man.

There was the sound of approaching footsteps. A young man in a dark blue sweater and worn blue cotton trousers came down the companion-way with his head cocked slightly to one side. He had the friendly open face of a young farm boy, which was slightly marred by spots but still made a wholesome impression. Above his forehead, as a result of his lank hair being combed straight back, a fluffy border had formed where hairs had been pulled out and were now growing back, such as one finds with many lads in smithies or bike stores.

'This is our helmsman,' said the hoarse man. The young fellow sat down and began slurping his tea. At the back of his neck, just above the collar of his sweater, he had a huge boil, which explained why he carried his head on one side.

'You're growing horns,' said the cook.

'He's got them already,' said the man with the cousin at teacher training college.

'You're right,' said the young man, feeling the swollen area, wincing but still with tender movements.

'Disease is a killer,' said the man with the cousin.

A dispute then ensued on the question of whether it was advisable to try treating it oneself and, for example, doing a little amateur surgery.

'If we're still stuck here tomorrow, I'll go to the doctor,' said the helmsman.

'You've got to sweat it out,' said the cook.

'Oh yeah, till he snuffs it,' observed the hoarse man. 'Don't you play doctor. You'll be kicking the bucket yourself any day now.'

It emerged from the ensuing discussion that the cook suffered from a liver complaint. There was a lively exchange of experiences and facts relating to doctors' diagnoses, conversations in waiting rooms, inefficient, careless or quite maliciously inappropriate treatment, the way in which, from the colour and degree of cloudiness of someone's water, one could deduce the state of their health, insurance, sick benefit and repayment for medicines. When these topics were exhausted, the cook, pointing to me, asked, 'Is he eating here?'

'No, you're right,' the hoarse man replied. 'I was to say that this gentleman was to go forward for his meal.'

'That'll be fun for him,' said the cook. At the same time he raised his head and listened intently. 'They're at it again!' he exclaimed. From a loudspeaker in the direction of the lounge, faint but distinctly audible, came the sound of an organ. 'Right, come on,' said the cook, jumping up. He went into the cabin where the accordion lay, took hold of it and came back to the table where he began squeezing the instrument violently in and out, holding down as many bass notes at once as possible. The accordion, at full volume, gave a series of breathless, deep shrieks.

'Stop it now,' said the helmsman, reaching out.

'Play us a nice tune then,' said the cook, handing him the instrument.

'No, not now,' said the lad, nevertheless slipping the straps over his elbows. He listened. The sound of the organ stopped. Then the lad began playing softly, but the others roared as loud as they could:
Tada of Montevideo...

I got up, asked the time for form's sake and went out. The ship was indeed lying in the mud, just behind the locks, some distance from the shore. The gap was too wide for a gangplank. For this reason a wooden ladder had been put out, one end of which was attached to the bottom of the railings and the other rested on an island-shaped clump of grass about half a metre from the shore. The rain had almost stopped, but the wind had increased to gale force.

In the lounge the table had been set for a cold buffet for three. The radio had been turned off, but the cabinet was still open and the Bible lay on the table. We sat down.

'Have you been back there?' asked the captain, pointing to the stern.

'Yes, I walked round a bit,' I confessed. His wife observed the movements of his face closely. He said nothing else. They both proceeded to prayer. Then we began eating in silence.

'Are you married?' asked the woman, after I had passed her the butter dish.

'Yes,' I replied. 'I've been married for five years.'

The captain looked up. 'What are you going to do in London?' he asked. I started explaining in a roundabout way that I was learning English so as to be able to write in English. The longer I went on, the more stupid and mendacious my statements seemed. My face was burning again, and apart from that my nose had become blocked.

'Do you go to church often?' asked the woman.

'No, not so often actually,' I replied. I wanted to say something accommodating. 'Sometimes, if someone in the family gets married or something, occasionally,' I said.

The captain gave no visible reaction, but a couple of quick muscular twitches passed over the woman's face, so that for a moment she seemed to be about to smile. But she simply pursed her lips more firmly.

'When they need God, yes, then they go to church,' she said, and cast an imperious glance at her husband.

'You needn't pay too much attention to that lot,' he said suddenly, pointing to the stern. It was not quite clear what he meant. 'Or else, if you must find it worthwhile listening to them, you must make up your own mind.'

'Of course it's your own affair,' said the woman, her eyes were fixed on her husband.

'If you like you can go and sit with them for the whole crossing,' said the husband, without looking at me.

We finished the meal in silence.

'Cards, cards! Nothing but cards!' said the woman, turning back to me. 'Weren't they playing cards?'

'No, I didn't see them,' I replied.

'I can't forbid them,' said the captain.

'I'm not so sure you can't forbid them,' said the woman, putting her hands in her lap. Again she looked at her husband, and waited for him to say something, but he remained silent. 'God's hand is upon this ship,' she said. 'And what Elder Hommes said the other day.'

'Aren't the signs of God's wrath to be found everywhere?' asked the captain, looking sharply at me.

'Yes, of course,' I replied.

'God warns us daily,' he went on. 'For we are God's angels.'

'That storm at sea,' the woman continued, 'was that just a coincidence?'

I just looked serious and said nothing. The captain read the next chapter from the Bible. After the prayer, I stayed sitting for a moment. I still had my overcoat with me. I could go to my cabin now, but if I wanted to go back on deck I would have go through the lounge again. I went on deck climbed on all fours down the ladder to the shore, and walked into the village. The shop had not yet closed and I purchased an envelope and writing paper, went to the Zeepost pub, had a glass of gin, wrote a short letter home, bought a stamp that because of the insane wind I had to take out of the tray of the machine with great caution, and posted the letter. I decided to stay out for as long as possible, so that when I got back on board I could go straight to bed without causing resentment. A stroll on the pier was impossible because of the violence of the storm. So I just walked aimlessly round for a while. For some reason the sight of the houses and streets where there was absolutely nothing of interest was deeply depressing. I went back on board at about eight o'clock. Only the captain was left in the lounge. In order to avoid any misunderstanding I told him that I had been for a walk, and asked him about the chances of putting to sea.

'Maybe tonight,' he replied. 'Or tomorrow morning.' For a moment it seemed a conversation might develop, but his face clouded over again and he looked at me with such suspicion that I quickly disappeared to my cabin.

In the stern the accordion playing continued for another hour. Then everything on board went quiet. Stumbling steps on the companion-way next to mine indicated that the captain was also going to bed. I thought about reading, but could not find anything worthwhile in my luggage. Apart from that, the sparse light of the ceiling lamp turned books and all printed matter into something unreal and futile. The water lapped loudly against the hull of the ship, occasionally drowned out by the howling gusts of wind. I was assured of twelve hours of peace and quiet, for the time being I no longer needed to be on my guard against anything, but I did not feel in the least relaxed or safe. I sat there, fully dressed, on the edge of the bunk, staring at the floor. The strange space I found myself in, the wind, the lighted windows of houses still just visible in the distance, on the other side of the canal where people lived whom I would never know, the sound of distant ships' sirens, all pointed to a wasted existence, a messed-up life, and thinking about all this was bound to lead to the evocation of such deep sadness that even the desire to jerk off would vanish. 'What a state,' I said aloud. 'What bullshit. Go to bed.' I rocked to and fro, still sitting on the bunk, and shook my head. 'O Lord, willst Thou not speak to my Conditions?' came into my head. I listened, but God did not speak. The usual whirl of memories did, though, start up again, never more than shreds, half-finished sentences, voices, nonsensical statements by teachers, uncles and aunts from the provinces waffling in dialect, youth group leaders or small shopkeepers, which may or may not have been made one afternoon in or near a garden or a downstairs flat. God only knew. Silence that inspires. Faces too, lots of them, floating up from the depths, full of angry features, clearly with something to say, but without uttering any sound. This time, God be praised, they were all dead, all dumb for evermore, and could never again pester me with their casuistry and futile arguments. That was at least some consolation. Among them was the face of a boy from a summer camp, who at night in the tent, at least twenty years ago, had read aloud before bedtime from a book in which it said that some stars were so far away that their light took thousands of years to reach our earth, and who after the lamp was blown out was given a good hiding by the camp leader,

and later was beaten to death in a German camp, since I remembered having heard some report or mention of it somewhere. God
sent signs and warnings, perhaps.

The Gift

A Persian Fairy Tale

Harry Mulisch

translated by Paul Vincent

'Very well, very well, very well,' sighed the caliph with a wave of the hand. 'Show him in.'

The grand vizier bowed and disappeared. That same instant the caliph had forgotten the name of the emir who had come to pay his respects. Since he had united the kingdom, they all came to pay their respects, sometimes three in one day. He had never dreamed that he had brought together so many sheikhs and sultans under his dominion.

Unification had not been a simple matter. He had begun when he was only twenty-five, in the name of the Prophet of course, and he was now sixty-five. First he had tackled Tabriz. Quite a few heads had rolled there, as they had too shortly afterwards in Heriz, Ahar, Mehriban and Sarab. Once it was calm and quiet as the grave in those parts, he had turned his attention to Hamadan. In Bijar there had been that incident with the thirty-six babies. He himself did not remember it with any pride, but when the Inshilas showed no signs of wanting to moderate their moral indignation, he had been more or less obliged to go there. One thing led to another. With the best will in the world he could not avoid Tusharkan, with a sideswipe he pacified Malayer, and the fact that Kurds got caught in the middle was not really his fault. A great deal of blood had been shed, it had to be said, albeit not as much as later in Kesan and Kirman, to say nothing of Kum and Mashhad. Looking back, it would have been better if those people from Luristan had never got involved, all historians were agreed on that, since then a few might have been left alive, which was now not really the case. What a nuisance, looking back at all that. Shiraz, Afshar, Kaskai, Abadeh and the Prophet knew where else: bloodbaths, rape, fire, devastation, it was all mixed up in his memory. All things considered his life had been one long grind.

And to think that as a boy he had looked forward to torturing. But what had he in fact seen? That suffering renders man innocent. A fine trick life had played on him! All those enemies that he had tortured into angels! By Allah, that had never been his intention. And all in all, why was he so dead set on uniting the kingdom? For the power? Yes, he had that now. If he moved his little finger, that changed people's lives somewhere; if he so much as raised an eyebrow, that was the end of them. But what was it that he now had? What use was power actually? If man were immortal, power would mean something. All things considered seeing as in a hundred years' time everyone, the mighty included, would be six feet under, striving for power was nothing but a waste of time. And if it was the power to kill that gave satisfaction, then it should at least make one immortal: not in books, but in the flesh! What was more ridiculous than a dead potentate? What more moving than someone dead and powerless?

The caliph sighed. After all, everything always turned out wrong in life. All he had really achieved, was to wreck his sleep and his dreams. As soon as he sank into the pillows at night and wanted to leave the kingdom to its own devices, they all reared their heads again: the ones from Tabriz and Heriz and Ahar, the ones from Bijar, Keshan, Kirman and Luristan – all of them. And finally, invariably, the thirty-six babies, turned partly inside out like slaughtered lambs in the market, their eyes red as poppies. There was no going to sleep after that, but that wasn't all: the crescent hung in the sky like a scimitar dripping with blood, and in the deserts the hyenas howled like the dying. Not until first light did everything calm down. When he saw it had all been just imagination, he fell into an unpleasant sleep, so deep and compact that when he awoke he had difficulty opening his swollen eyes.

In the shade the carpets glowed, the perfumes gave off their scent. Outside, water babbled through the hot afternoon. From the harem came a faint giggling and somewhere in a corner a fly buzzed. The grand vizier opened the tapestries.

'Emir al-Muktafi, lord.'

Nose to the ground, like an anteater, the emir crept in.

'Look up, friend,' said the caliph. 'I can't see your mug like that.'

'May the blessing of Allah be with you, king of kings.'

'May be? What do you mean: may be? Isn't it certain then?'

'Of course,' said the emir, turning pale, 'without a doubt, darling of the Prophet. Even the birds and butterflies in your kingdom know that.'

'Yes, yes, we know all about that,' said the caliph. 'The birds and the butterflies... ' He chortled for a moment and then asked: 'Where are you from and why have you come? I probably won't be able to grant your request.'

'I'm from Luristan, mighty ruler.'

'From Luristan?' repeated the caliph in surprise. 'What's this? Are there people alive there then?'

'Undeservedly, incomparable light of mankind, undeservedly. A few cowardly, scurvy dogs managed to escape your righteous anger and returned without honour. They now work the land contemptibly but peacefully and no longer concern themselves with politics.'

'Oh?' said the caliph bending forward a little. 'So I don't enter into their thoughts?'

The emir now turned as white as his burnous.

'Their thoughts centre *entirely* on you, right hand of Allah, precisely because you stand above politics like the eagle above the chicken coop.'

'A very sensible view,' nodded the caliph, leaning back.

'We ask your forgiveness for the unforgivable churlishness with which we worms continue to breathe and contaminate the air that is rightfully yours alone.'

The caliph made a weary gesture with his hand to indicate that it was all right.

'We humbly beg you,' said the emir, 'to accept our impudent and unworthy gift.'

'Aha,' said the caliph, 'a gift. And what might that be?'

The emir produced a red vase from under his burnous and placed it on the rug.

'A worthless vase, cherishing sun of the faithful.'

The caliph and the emir looked at the wine-red vase, which for a moment stood at the centre of the kingdom. The fountain in the garden babbled, but a hush had fallen over the harem. The emir did not dare to look up at the caliph and to his alarm saw a large blue-bottle alight on the vase with disgusting, tacky movements. It struck him as a bad omen. Fortunately the fly was on his side and, breathing as carefully as possible, he tried not to disturb it. He praised Allah that the fly gave no sign of wanting to venture across the vase, which would bring it into the vision of the caliph, who might then interpret the omen in his own way. Healthy and content it sat rubbing its legs and made the occasional rapid movement as if washing its neck.

'Nice vase,' said the caliph. 'Definitely. Thank you very much. What the – '

And only the caliph saw how at the precise moment of that 'Thank you very much', as it changed owners, the vase also changed colour: from wine red to blood red. But at the same moment only the emir saw the fly fall dead on the carpet.

Sugar

Hugo Claus

translated by PC Evans

The washery's steam whistle blew. 'There 'ee goes,' said Lambert
sleepily. He'd already stuck it out for an hour, lying pressed up
against the ice-cold concrete floor, motionless, while the cold must
have been penetrating to his bones, right through his khaki trousers
and gum boots. In the mornings this elegant lad wouldn't stick in
any straw like the rest of us because of the office girls. Every day,
before our shift finished, it was the same old game. Suddenly, he'd
spring up top three steps at a time, then he'd stand with his hands
on his hips, curls blowing in the wind, his treacherous head pointing in my direction, bobbing up and down in front of the office
where the French girls were weighing up the first cart-loads. Till
now though they'd probably felt he was too thin, too pale. So far
(this was the third month of the season) he hadn't found one
prepared to do anything with him in practice, and he jawed our ears
off about it every evening, until even the bog warden, who we'd
nick-named Hotty, started getting fed up. Lambert looked at me; his
one eye closed and swollen beneath the white bandage that ran
slanting across his forehead. A neckerchief around his chin, a
bandage around his head, elbow nearly broke, that's what you ended
up with if you came too close to Block 2, where all the Poles drank
together in the evenings.

They'd given him a hiding, the Zribowskis, Pichevskis or whatever they were called and, if it hadn't been for Heinrich and Max,
Lambert would not have got back to our barracks and been able to
say panting, in the reedy voice of a boy who's been shaken up, his
head bleeding: 'Unbelievable, that filthy crew in those huts over
there, not one of them makes his bed, and they just chuck potato
peelings, egg shells, empty packets onto the floor and it stinks of just
about everything, and you slip on, oh, all sorts of gunk,' and here he
turned bright red and mumbled a few words to himself, which no
one could understand. We knew that the Poles didn't wash, and they
let their stubble grow all through the season because they were lazy,
so they looked like bark with red patches for faces, but about it being
so awful in their huts, which they didn't let anyone inside of, yes, we
all ought to take a look at that some time. That's what was etched on
the silent faces of the Flemings, half stretched out on their beds,
trying to imagine how filthy it could be over there, among the Polaks.

Once more the steam whistle.

I raised the hose higher so the water spurted out in an arc in
front of the bottom row of beets. Lambert went to see if the beets
weren't jammed in the tunnel.

'More water,' he screamed.

I pointed the hose straight into the channel. It gushed over and
suddenly ran almost empty. The beets had jammed the tunnel and
now they rapidly flowed on further.

I burrowed out the mountain in front of me once again. The
brown water hollowed out the pyramid of beets, groping into every
cranny in the pink, white wall of heaped beets, gnawing into the
lowest layers, until the wall finally had to collapse.

I'd had it up to my eyeteeth, staring all night into a gutter of
surging beets.

The tap on the hose was really tight and every time I needed to
switch direction a cold gust of air blew up my soaking gloves and
over my chapped fingers. The water seeped into my boots. 'The
factory should have given us diving suits for work like this,' I'd said
to Lambert about twenty times already and every time he'd laughed
with disdain. He chucked a beet on the floor in front of me. It was
his turn to hose now; I could go and help out in the washery.

When he leant on the tap with his wrecked elbow, manoeuvring the hose with a painful face, I asked him if Richard had already stowed away his sugar.

'No, not yet,' he said, 'but keep an eye on him.'

Heinrich came to look. His small silhouette above the iron railing resembled a green, mouldy statue. As if he were still a sentinel, a guardian of the Eternal Kingdom, with his threadbare uniform and his boots and his Tyrolese cap. I asked him if Richard had already stowed away his sugar.

But a shrill, angry voice called out to him from close by: 'Einrick – Einrick'.

Richard popped up, swore and said that Heinrich was a *voyou*, and that he hadn't lost anything around the hose and that everything was going to hell in the washery. The German answered, shook his head at us briefly and left.

'Eh, Hugo,' Richard called.

The night was thick and cold, it pierced every fibre of the men there. The voices were hoarse and unfriendly, the noise and roar of the factory ominous.

I walked across the slanting concrete floor, kicked the scattered beets into the gutter, and followed them with my eyes as they splashed into the brown water. Then I climbed up on top. Richard tugged his cap down, till it was right over his eyebrows, below which there were two glassy eyes floating in a yellow fluid.

'Hugo,' he said, and I thought he was going to start bawling, he looked so pitiful, so abandoned by everyone, *'fais attention à ces voyous d'allemands.'* He tried to walk on, his one hand held on tightly to the depot railing. I said to his back that I'd do just that, right away even, and I waited till he'd gone past the railway-wagons and Pjotr's oxen and then followed after him.

Pjotr meandered along in the light of a lantern. He tapped his finger to his cap in silence, then trailed after the trundling, soundless, colossal yellow oxen, whose heads were lashed in the wooden yoke, swaying in the same direction, and whose horns, flanks and backs gleamed.

'Hu,' said Pjotr. It was a wondrous sound: 'Hu, hu,' and his tongue clicked. The night was leaden, and the only discernible sound was the chinking of the oxen's chains and the dry snap of Pjotr's whip. How many days to go?

For a moment I thought that Richard was throwing up against one of the railway-wagons, but then he straightened up again and I carried on following about three or four metres behind him, I could see that he was finally lugging his sugar now. He was all hunched up, as though he'd acquired an enormous, grey hump. He dictated my pace by his. We walked in step through the grey night, as though in a church, the pillars of which were chimneys; the arches, clouds. From our room, a beam of light shone across the pump, the forks and the puddles of water on the ground, which might serve as altar light.

I thought: 'Why doesn't Richard light our way with a torch? I'll be bumping into him at this rate.'

How much can a man steal? Who should a man steal from? Do you have to be sure first that someone has more than you?

Richard was dragging his sack of sugar along the ground now, through the cook's garden. I waited, leaning against the Germans' hut.

Richard had enough sugar. He had a top class job. All of the best jobs went to the French. Which was fair enough. Natives first! What did Richard do actually? Run a washery, where he didn't even know exactly how the beets got washed, stroll around in his clogs, nice and warm, sometimes have the Germans polish a machine (which they had to yank cobbles out of, enough to lay a new street from the factory to the village). And, after the controller had been by, around one or two o'clock, he'd go and pick up his sack of sugar, which the native-stokers had put away for him, while he happily downed the four bottles of wine he'd brought from home, punctuated by cups of harmful, white, diluted alcohol and sugar. And when he was nicely warmed up, purple, sweating and bloated on the stuff, he'd give the steam whistle a little toot, so that the two people on the hose, in the freezing night, might shift their lazy bodies.

When the daylight touched the apex of the pyramids and brightened the lamplight from the lime kilns, every beet, clump of earth, pale beet root and the gluey goo in the trough, like so many ores from a mountain landscape from God knows where, when the lamplight blanched its groping fingers, then, yes, that's when I trudged to our room with Richard's twenty kilos of sugar and Lambert's twenty.

The day shift was still sleeping. Only one of the Vincke brothers (Leon or Gaston, I could only tell them apart with some difficulty, especially now that they'd both taken out their teeth and popped them in the same glass of water, and both of them had the same striped blue shirts on) cried from behind my back: '*Crapule*'.

But when I spun around with a whipping motion, they were both still asleep, or at least they acted like they were. I shook the nearest one's shoulder. It was Leon, the sixty-two year old. 'Hey,' I said, but he scrunched up his dark blue eyelids with their dozens of wrinkles even tighter, and pursed his lips. He looked like a fourteen-day-old corpse.

'Filthy skunk,' I whispered close to his ear.

I glanced over the row of beds, waited, held my breath, but the workers from the day shift didn't stir. I poured out the slithering, white, powdered sugar into my pillow and Lambert's, and crumbled up the lumps with my fingers and hammered a couple of hollows into it for my head.

Old Vincke would probably be too lazy to get up and drag away the pillows. But I couldn't say for sure.

'Oh, if only the morning would hurry over the factory buildings and the fields and over the world and over all the people I'm driving beets to the factory for,' I sang to myself. I stood with the hose beneath the useless light of the lamps, gnawing away at the pyramids like a rat, the hose washing away mountains, and then the first of the farm-carts pulled up.

The farmers cried to their horses, and to us: '*Bonjour, Flemings*' over the shrieks of the iron lime-wagons, and the gushing of the hose.

Now and then, one of them would clamber down off his cart and stand nodding his crafty head next to us, asking how it was going, saying it'd be warmer than yesterday, and that the factory ripped off the farmers.

'And not us!' we said. He nodded and rolled a cigarette, yawning at the beets floating by.

Just before eight the Germans always came in a little early to relieve us, wearing their Tyrolese caps, and their gleaming water-proof suits, which they'd got in the army to protect them from phosphorus bombing.

When we trudged through the field with the sugar on our shoulders, Lambert, his pale face drawn, said: 'I'm going to Compiègne tomorrow. He held his white head-bandage tight and sang: 'Where all the girls are'.

'There're some here as well, aren't there.'

'What in God's name do you think of me? That I'd go round with those women, who haven't washed for a year, who reek of Germans, Poles, French, Yugoslavs, Australians, Tierra del Feugans...'

I looked straight ahead, at the glistening rails, as far as the flat fallow land, with no seed or fruit, as far as the swamps.

'... Chinese, Eskimos...'

As though the women from the village – who all came to the same well to draw water, in their black scarves and black stockings, who really never washed, but who were warm, God-fearing and generous, who'd already lived six or seven lives – as though they'd been born more than a hundred years ago on Tierra del Feugo or in Sydney. As though they had played out the same game then as they did here and now, seducing the men and going down on their backs with hope in their shadowed eyes, unaware of their fate after their first death, which would deliver them up to the young Flemings, with their elongated stingers pointing out at them, in the stench of this French village.

And what would we be blessed with if tomorrow perhaps, after Lambert or I had fallen into the channel with our drunken bones and were swept away with the flood of beets, and ended up through the tunnel and inside the first grinding bin at the washery, as had happened with an old French man two years earlier? In what form would we come back? Man, plant, dirt?

Lambert walked on ahead, he still held his bandage tight with one hand; he walked like a farmer's son, with a loping stride.

Straight across the stubble fields. Barren, plucked land, where hay cocks were scattered everywhere. And vaguely, in the distance, a flat horizon, forming an arch like the sea. Not a single tree.

Steppe, Arctic tundra, pampas.

The earth formed crusts beneath our boots. Here and there, soiled paper wafted up on the breeze. Belonging to the Germans. Who didn't dare use the factory toilets, or at least that's what

Heinrich reckoned. Often, when evening fell and Heinrich, Lambert and I went rowing on the Oise, rowing in the thickening silence, the oars dipping inaudibly in the water, the boat shifting inaudibly further, the sounds of the evening resonating as if in a great room, we'd see their crouched figures spread all over the field. Still with their caps on.

'The Cripple's got two daughters,' Lambert said quietly, 'one of them's a dream.'

'To get your sheets wet.'

And then we arrived, dropped the sacks down, brushed our sweat off. The Cripple had clearly not been awake for long because he came padding up in his shirtsleeves, his bare feet in his clogs, tugging at the ends of his moustache nervously. His left shoulder was raised, which made him look like a sick raven.

In the kitchen there were pieces of furniture, flour and sugar sacks, pitchforks, shovels, three mattresses and I don't know how many cushions in a pile. There he strode back and forth. He asked if anybody had seen us coming in and then cleared a path through the middle of his household wares, kicking a few pots and pans aside, turning over some chairs so that we could get to the depot with our sacks of sugar.

After he'd paid us our money, which we divvied up straight away, he turned the chairs upright again. He dragged a couple of mattresses in front of the door to the depot. Then he stood in front of us, hesitant, his fat fingers with their cleft knuckles groping along the collar of his shirt and into his grey curls.

'If there's ever any of those big, blue cans...' he said. His wrinkled face below the fringe of white hair resembled a Greek philosopher, but I couldn't remember which one. Though it would have been really difficult to spirit those petrol cans out of the hanger, we still nodded and talked prices.

Then Lambert whispered: 'Hey, Cripple, where's your daughters?'

The Cripple looked at him with contempt, then flung himself into a total pantomime routine, raising his eyebrows, and sticking out his bottom lip, he made a 'Pff' sound, 'Pff' with his moist lower lip, on which bubbles of saliva formed.

'They're still asleep,' he said, and hooked his fingers into his shirt again. He leaned over. 'The cans…'

'Let's have a look at your daughters,' I said.

He touched a deathly-straight finger to his mouth, and it seemed like he'd grown a trunk. We followed after him on tiptoe, in the trail of the hot, dungy scent of his body. And when we could look inside I whistled very softly. (As only I could, with a short puff of air through the gap in my teeth.)

There were his two daughters lying pressed up against each other in a very high, old bed. The one with the dark curls carried on sleeping, grumbling for a moment, but the other sat up straight in bed.

She had a brown, crooked face. I could only guess at the petite shoulders, the collarbones, the pear-shaped breasts beneath the red, threadbare pullover. She was about eighteen. '*Merde, ah, merde alors*,' she said laughing as she rubbed her eyes.

We stuck our heads in through the door, the Cripple walked on ahead, and as he bowed he made a sweeping gesture with his arm, so that his raised shoulder turned into a wing, which furled out.

'*Voici Jacqueline, ma fille*,' the raven cawed.

The daughter carried on rubbing her eyes, then she crept back beneath the sheets, close up to her sister, and she winked.

'*Bonjour, Messieurs*,' she said, like a very young girl. She rolled over onto her stomach and buried her face in the ragged, grey pillows. The Cripple walked us as far as the gate. It had grown colder and the Cripple was hopping back and forth. Soon he had to go because he had the shits. I wished it on him.

'So, don't forget the cans. Two thousand francs,' he said. We walked down the gravel path, alongside the land with its ochre pleats.

Only the electric pylons at the factory rose into the air, growing out of this winterland.

'Do you reckon that she had anything on under that pullover?' Lambert asked. 'I'd have thought he might have lifted the blankets up for once, after all the sugar we've brought him.'

'So that you could see the mole on her backside. And what then?

But when we were out in the open field, unprotected, the cold morning descended on us, its icy darts attacking my warm body. Like a woman, licking my knees, my thighs. I quivered, stuck my hands in my pockets. Then the first rays of the sun struck and made the puddles on the beet field glisten. There was a red veil over the slanting horizon.

'The sun looks like an open vagina as it rises,' I thought, 'immersing us in its heat. Like a gigantic goddess spreading her vagina; holding us captive with her red splendour.'

'Look,' someone said with a piercing, fearful voice, 'look and see if you can spot the womb. After three days it hangs down lower, if it's been fertilised. Then later, it's drawn back up again.'

'I can see,' I said.

'What can you see?' Lambert asked. He looked cheerful with his face wrecked. He was pleased with the money in his pockets.

'Compiègne. Ah, Compiègne,' he said.

Lambert couldn't get the doors open. I heard him screaming something vicious, and the sound of metallic blows ringing out in the furious night. They were those old-fashioned, French railway-wagons, and you could hammer on the handles for half an hour with an iron bar without the doors moving a centimetre. Then, suddenly, inexplicably, on the last unexpected strike the doors would fly open as if they'd been softened up. And you had to make sure you got out of the way fast.

'It's not working. Point your hose to the left,' Lambert cried nervously. Not a single beet flowed through the channel and the steam whistle had already sounded from the washery twice. I changed direction, and the water spurted against the hanger, where the rusty plates and the pins glistened. The blows resumed, and then Heinrich appeared as well; he'd probably been sent from the washery. I could tell it was Heinrich hammering on the handles because of the regular, hard tone, and the rapidity of the blows. Lambert might hit as hard, but sporadically, in salvos, depending on his mood. And he tired quickly too.

'Bwwanggg.' I pointed the hose into the railway-wagon and saw Heinrich and Lambert jump out of the way of the flood of beets and the water splashing and gushing through the door.

Heinrich climbed up on top.

'There are no more beets in the washery,' he said. He came up next to me and sat down on a side-beam.

'Richard's furious,' he said. Heinrich carried out his work at the washery conscientiously, as all of the Germans working at the factory did. Most of them had signed a contract as 'free *arbeiders*', and they took this as a grave and serious obligation. If they'd worked consistently for a year, they were allowed to go home. Sometimes even before the prisoners of war.

'Ludwig's going home next week,' Heinrich said.

'How many are there still ahead of him?'

'Ah,' said Heinrich, 'first there's Heinz, who's nearly sixty, then Ludwig, whose wife's expecting a baby...'

'How can that be possible?'

Heinrich looked straight past me, into the shadows of our tumbledown shed, to the hay, the strewn clothes, the flour sacks. He rolled a cigarette, and said: 'Maybe his wife did it on purpose, so he'd be allowed home? Maybe Ludwig even asked her to? Who knows? What a man won't do?

I hosed out the last corner. The beets bounced into the channel like pink, stiff, dead, creatures. The water, gleaming in the yellow lamplight lay in the railway-wagons, seeping slowly through the cracks in the plank floor.

'After that, it'll be Max's turn, he's got three kids. Then me, with a wife and two children. *Ja ja.*' (The cryptic, German '*ja ja*', that sounded like a complaint). 'Ludwig'll probably be leaving this week. They had a party last night.'

I knew what it would have been like. They'd have sat there together on their beds drinking wine gravely, silently, singing their songs in a choir and duet. No one yelling or shouting out anything cheerful or dancing. They'd have sat there straight in the shadowy room with their invariably freshly laundered shirts and trousers, singing or talking about home in their terse, bitten-off, gruff sentences. Like grey beetles in hibernation.

Heinrich offered me a half-rolled cigarette. I licked the edge and he finished it off and gave me a light.

'Ho,' Lambert yelled from outside and a new railway-wagon shunted beneath our feet. Once more the metallic blows tore the hubbub and din of the factory apart.

'Lambert's much too nervy,' Heinrich said.

'And too weak,' I replied. We laughed. Then he pursed his lips again and said: 'I don't get it'.

Three weeks earlier in the late afternoon we'd gone to a fortune-teller in Compiègne because Heinrich didn't dare to go on his own. The fortune-teller, who was a coarse woman of around forty, left the room every now and then to quieten someone moaning in the next room (a patient, a feverish child, a dying mother?): '*Tais-toi, j'ai des clients*', saying with an unfathomable look that we weren't French, that we had good characters, and how we worked at the sugar factory. Then she laid her fingers on the photo of Heinrich's wife, a southern face, with a broad, masculine mouth. She placed the photo down among the cards and began the game.

'Oeioeioei,' she moaned; she stated with some concern that Heinrich's wife still hadn't deceived him, though there was a white man close by who was deceiving her, and the best thing for Heinrich to do would be to go home.

'I don't get it.'

Heinrich spoke in his raw Mecklenburg accent and I had to guess at the meaning of half the words, which he only muttered to himself: 'Not even when I was eighteen, or twenty, the age when all the others chase after women. It wasn't normal, they said. I've had two wives, and the first of them was for twelve years, and I never messed around with anyone else. Everything went to that one woman, that one body, that one (*einzige, einzige, einzige*) thing I knew, that I really knew. And it was only when she died that I took another wife, and she meant just the same to me. Not the same, but the same a second time round. In America in 1943, I had a good job as a barman in an officer's mess. If there were any women still around at 3am, they'd ask me to dance. I couldn't do it. What do you think that means? They say it's not normal. Perhaps not.'

I could picture Heinrich wandering around the heavily lit bar with its gleaming parquet floor, his trunk bobbing slowly and gently in a khaki uniform. His stern face with its tired eyes, shaking '*Nein*' at the nervous American women gathered around him at 4am, excited by the heat, the sweat, the dancing, the alcohol and the proximity of this strangely calm enemy. Rubbing their firm, tense thighs up against the bar.

'Now I really want to go home soon,' said Heinrich. 'I'm afraid. Maybe something's happened already.'

'The white man close to her?'

'Maybe. I haven't heard anything from her in two months. Not since I left the camp in Arras. Max says the postmistress stops most of the German letters. Because her nephew was shot in front of a firing squad. Can that be true?'

'I don't think so.'

'In any case, she always gives me a sly look. Never talks to me. She calls the postmaster over whenever I'm in. Ahh,' he brushed his words away with a dismissive gesture. 'Bella gets more beautiful every day though,' he said.

I nodded. Bella was a naked lady that Lambert and I had carved in bas-relief into one of the beams in our hut, and to which we added a couple of finer details every night. Yesterday evening Lambert had coloured in her nipples with a lipstick. When the rest of us went back to Belgium Lambert wanted to saw the beam down and take Bella with him.

We called her Bella after Lambert's fiancée. If someone said: 'Her hips are too broad, or her legs too thin,' Lambert would say proudly: 'I'm the one who knows best how Bella should look. Her hips, and her legs and all the rest.'

'What'll you do when you get home, Heinrich?'

'I don't know. I can't think about it. I probably won't be able to play the piano any more. But maybe I could go into my brother's business. He died in Italy, and his wife hasn't re-married, and their house wasn't flattened.'

Why couldn't he play piano any more?

'There'll be no need of piano players in Germany,' he said, and shoved himself off the beam and went and stood at the peephole. He'd found his correct German again:

'The first week I was here I walked to Compiègne in my civvies one evening, fourteen kilometres on foot, and I played the piano there in a dance hall. Gershwin, Peter Kreuder, Strauss, and all of the French applauded like lunatics and yelled: *bis, bis*. Then after, at 5am, I walked back. Fourteen kilometres. I found it very hard going at first. I still do, sometimes, I get up at night and stand by the window and play on the window-sill.'

'Do you like Peter Kreuder?' I asked him.

'Hm... so so.'

'I like the song that Zarah Leander sang in *Paramatta*.'

'That's not by Peter Kreuder,' said Heinrich.

'Who's it by then?'

'I don't know. I've never seen the film. I've only seen two German films over the last five years, they were two old ones, from the mid 20s. It was in a museum in America, and I had to go with an American officer.'

'There're some really good ones.'

'I like Gustav Mahler most,' he said. 'His music's a lot better than Cole Porter's or Peter Kreuder's. It has a tragic sound to it.'

We listened to the water gurgling in the railway-wagons. Heinrich started singing softly. His eyes were half-closed and it was all too much, too familiar, too like a child's hand clutched around my throat, I tugged at the hose so that the water spurted in an arch against the sides of the train, and it rattled deafeningly.

Heinrich stopped. He tugged his cap down to the regulation position with that strange motion, which is the Germans' very own, as any good habit should be, like rolling cigarettes, or looking at a wristwatch. One: a little tug at the curved peak; two: smoothing back the hair above the ears with two or three fingers.

'I've got to go,' he said and touched my shoulder. 'We'll go to Compiègne together one day, and I'll play for you.'

'Yes, we'll do that,' I said. 'Bye, Heinrich.'

'Bye,' he said. He clambered down the iron ladder and shouted something to Lambert below. Then I heard him speaking to Pjotr, the ox handler. Lambert took over from me on the hose, and I went to lie in the hay, my frozen hands tucked between my thighs. An ice-cold wind pierced through the cracks in the plank floor and the hay. The whole shed shook every time Lambert changed direction with the hose. Far away, as always, the thunder of the washery. A wall of sound.

Verheiden came to take over from Lambert. He was the oldest of the Flemings. Seventy-two. He didn't do a thing in the factory, he just wandered around all day with a pitchfork over his shoulder, hoisted a beet every couple of hours and chucked it on the farmer's carts that were driving in and out. In the evenings he was in bed by eight, a scarf around his bald head like a turban, giving his commentary on the day that had just passed. Or endlessly telling stories about his life. When everyone from the day shift had fallen asleep, he'd still be talking in a croaky alcoholic voice in clipped sentences, which he repeated at intervals, like refrains from a heathen's prayer:

'In 1929 there was the blast. And rain too. *A tout casser.* We didn't have boots like you do now. Didn't have any boots. Didn't have any boots. And the oven blew. A Russian. A communist, they said. Yes, a Russian. And the women's skirts blew up as far as Saint-Denis. Blew right up they did. Blew right up. What a blast. What a terrible blast...'

And he went on like this till half eleven, twelve o'clock. Then the men from the night shift would come in and give him a slug of warm alcohol mixed with sugar from their flasks. He'd fall asleep, with a brief mutter.

I lay in the midst of the bitter-smelling hay as the pulsing, streaming water splashed into the railway-wagons in waves.

Suddenly there was shouting outside, a cry, and it didn't come from the factory or the machines or from the lime-wagons, and Lambert, who was on the hose, cried in an urgent voice: 'Hugo, something's happened to Heinrich.'

'Heinrich,' a German voice outside was shouting, and something else too. I jumped up and yelled through the peephole: '*Was ist los?*' Max, the cobbler, was waving his arms, he came running up to our cabin, his grey hairs flapping about his face like a medieval knight.

'Come quickly,' he yelled, 'Heinrich...' and then something else. He stayed standing where he was as he saw me clambering down the ladder. He shouted that I should go to Pjotr and he'd get a doctor. He ran across the courtyard with long booted legs between the small pyramids of beets.

I saw the shifting shadows of Pjotr's oxen behind the fourth or fifth railway-wagon.

'What is it?' Lambert called from the cabin, and screwed the nozzle of the hose tight. The water dripped softly from the mountains of beets like thick raindrops landing in puddles. I came up beside the oxen's yoke, and the chains dragged along the earth and clattered. 'Pjotr,' I called, 'Pjotr, *wo bist du?*'

He crept out of the shadows of the hangar, with his hunched-back and his sagging legs, crossing them as he set one foot in front of the other. His hair hung in his eyes, he leaned against a railway-wagon.

'*Der Heinrich*,' he said. '*Sehr, sehr schlecht.* Dead.'

'*Wo?*'

'*Ach, Gott*,' he sighed. He nodded his head and snorted: 'Dead. *Ja ja.*' I tugged at his sleeve. '*Wo?*'

'The ox. Not me,' he said and lifted his scabbed hand to his chest, and shook his yellow, Russian head with its lanky hair. He was very drunk. '*Ich so, da, da, hju, hju*, then the ox, hju, I not see *der Heinrich. Da*, the ox.'

Then he smirked. His teeth moved as he chewed. 'Ach,' he snorted and scratched his neck with the hand that held the ox whip tight.

I trailed after him, past the wagons, and then I saw Heinrich lying beneath the last one, with his arms flailed out and his head face up on the rail. I knelt beside him. There was no wound, no blood, no torn flesh to be seen. He lay there calmly, his grey eyes open, searching motionless for some constellation overhead, through the roof beams of the hangar. It was just that the wheel of the last railway-wagon had driven up almost as far as his navel. The wheel, with its metal sheen, was lodged impossibly high between his slightly parted thighs and the thick, green material of Heinrich's trousers, where everything must be shattered, pulverised.

'Heinrich,' I said and touched his cheek and his broad, almost unwrinkled forehead, which was still warm. Then he started to twitch at the mouth, and it fell open as if it was biting something. And then it remained open like a narrow, blue slit.

I stood up and picked up Heinrich's cap, which had fallen beside the rail, and said to Pjotr that he was dead.

'Dead?' Pjotr asked, as if he hadn't said the same thing a moment ago, as if I might have saved him, maybe by touching him, or speaking his name, as if I was now responsible.

'He tumbled backwards because of the impact of the bumper, over the rail, and then the wheel rode into him.'

Pjotr nodded.

'Wait. Max is coming with a doctor.'

'*Oh, ja*, perhaps Heinrich is not really dead.' He picked at his nose. All in all, he'd seen hundreds die in Russia and France. Or hadn't he? But this was different, a swift, metallic wheel of a death, pressing up between your thighs.

Max was circling around, flailing with his grey arms, yelling that there was no doctor, no night watchman. '*Eine Schande*,' he cried. In the washery the steam whistle blew. There were no more beets in the channel.

'*Merde, salaud*,' Max yelled over the courtyard. He repeated this three or four times and stamped his boot on the earth.

'What should we do?' asked Lambert, who didn't dare come any closer to Heinrich. Max couldn't be calmed. He danced with rage.

'*Eine Schande.* No doctor *und* no director. *Rien. Ah, cela ne se passera pas ainsi. Je ferai un rapport.*'

Then he came and stood close to me and a waft of that bitter beet scent that hangs on your clothes if you're in the washery for more than a quarter of an hour, swept over my face. For a moment he held his hand to the level of his chest. Did he want me to press there? His face was white, devastated.

'*Il est mort? Hein?*'

Again the steam whistle. I shouted to Lambert that he had to stay there and I climbed up top, and unscrewed the hose. I pulled it around to the other side of the cabin, because the railway-wagons probably wouldn't be driven away for the first couple of hours. The water spurted against the concrete wall. I bent forwards and held my head close to the leaden nozzle of the hose. The foaming water, the throbbing, hissing sound swept over me. Dry, protected, I sank beneath a waterfall.

Once again the steam whistle. The fourth time. An alarm for the approaching night train. A warning and a cry of distress from the factory's dark mass, to us, separate, scattered individuals in the fields, in the shadows of the termite hills.

The beets were jammed fast in the tunnel. It always happened when a new tunnel was being used, the beets from the last load stuck fast in the mud and dried and lodged there. Someone in a waterproof rubber suit came to the bottom of the ladder and looked at me.

'Ah, poor Ein-riek,' he said. I didn't answer. He walked off, awkward in his rubber trousers, and then he crept into the tunnel on his hands and knees like a gleaming new toy.

I hosed in a wide arch now, a full three metres above the rim of the channel. I'd grown a gigantic member, which I could piss with against the roofs, against the tops of the trees.

'Look, I'm pissing at the moon,' I cried to Lambert.

'They've taken him away,' he said. 'Pjotr has to go with the police. He wept like a child.' The toy emerged from the mouth of the tunnel, a gleaming, crawling insect, it stood up on its two hind legs, disappeared. The beets flowed.

'Yes. It's the fourth one this season. The two Poles. Abel's boy, and now Heinrich.'

'Abel's boy doesn't count,' said Lambert fiercely. He'd been there when the boy had climbed over three safety barriers and jumped into the open lime oven. I'd seen him a couple of times, Abel's boy. He could only speak with difficulty; from the age of twelve he'd been coming to work at the sugar factory with his father, had drunk the white alcohol mixed with sugar every day.

'That was no accident,' said Lambert. 'That was his own fault. He went looking for it.'

'Maybe it was Heinrich's fault too. What was he doing behind those wagons anyway?'

'Idiot,' said Lambert and walked away. I saw him a couple of minutes later standing by the director's car. I chased the stray beets that were popping up. I hadn't even listened to Heinrich when he was singing. Another four hours to go, then I'd sleep.

When Lambert and I were back in the hut again and Lambert was lying in the hay (not making a start on Bella) we talked about the end of the season, about the wages in the metalworks in Verviers, where most of the seasonal workers went in the winter. We didn't talk about Heinrich any longer. We'd do that later, in two or three days.

'What's that?' Lambert asked.

'The Germans,' I said. A procession was crossing the courtyard beneath the yellow lamplight. The Germans were leaving the sugar factory with slow steps in rows of three. They had their long field coats on with their shoulder straps. I could see that Max, who'd been a sergeant, was wearing his medals. They raised their stiff arms as high as their chests and kept their heads fixed firmly in one direction.

The Frenchman who was standing on the ladder below called to us: *'C'est la garde'*.

'The honour guard,' said Lambert.

Then Max's voice rang out, barking its orders over the raging noise, and they came to a halt, and one by one they entered the watchman's cabin, where Heinrich lay.

Memories of a Fox-Hunter

Willem van Toorn

translated by PC Evans

And now, as I look up from my writing, these memories also seem
like reflections in a glass, reflections which are becoming more and
more easy to distinguish. Sitting here, alone with my slowly
moving thoughts, I rediscover many little details, known only to
myself, details otherwise dead and forgotten with all who shared
that time.
Siegfried Sassoon, Memoirs of a Fox-Hunting Man

The landscape, thought Leeman, seemed like a drawing in a children's book: too beautiful, too stylised to the perfection of
gently-rolling hills with hedgerows and clusters of trees in autumn
colours, and the silvery loop of a stream. He had been travelling
through this southern English countryside for two weeks now, visit-
ing stately homes and villages ruined by modernisation, clogged
with carpet emporia and Olde Tea Shoppes, and public schools out
of the *Boys' Own* books of his youth; he had tried to differentiate the
dialects by which society's strata unerringly identified themselves
and each other; he had been following in the footsteps of a dead
minor poet and finally he'd ended up here, with the oddly poignant

feeling that he recognised a place that he'd certainly never been.

No, a school picture book, Leeman thought. You could imagine the fox in the shadows beneath a tree, with its tongue hanging out of its mouth, its front paw resting on a trapped rabbit, stuffed and mounted for the person drawing it. Where was the photographer meant to start with a landscape like this and still make sure that it didn't end up in the paper looking like snapshots out of the brochure: *The Garden of England?*

Perhaps this feeling of poignancy wasn't aroused by the landscape, but by its associations with other landscapes that the peace evoked – the river-country of his childhood summer holidays, the dew-speckled grass in his grandfather's orchard. He wondered if this was why he travelled: not so much to see new things but to find impulses for memories. To transform landscapes into memories.

He leant against the door of the Land Rover and lit a cigarette, but after two puffs he hastily stubbed it out again, because the game warden, who was leaning on the steering wheel in the car, glanced at the smoke disapprovingly. On the way here the old man had mentioned that a fox's map is made up of scents.

The car was parked at the edge of a grassy field, in the lee of a thick hedge. The land in front of them dropped to a stream in a valley. The country house where the hunt had begun early that morning, was on the hill opposite. It had a reddish tiled roof with a wonderful array of chimneys. Leeman could make out the white stripe of the drive and the overgrown forms of what had once been a French garden. They had been received on the steps eight hours earlier by a little old man in a tweed jacket, who had obligingly posed for the photographer, leaning elegantly on his walking stick, and who had taken them into a bleak salon full of portraits and dark old furniture, where the three of them had drunk a glass of port at eight o'clock in the morning at a table decked with books, letters and bottles. Leeman always remembered a moment on every journey when he thought: How in Christ's name did I end up here? On this journey it was the moment when the old gentleman had raised his glass in a toast to the dead writer. Preceding that there was a complex journey that could no longer be reconstructed, beginning with Leeman's fascination for the writer, Siegfried Sassoon, and of which Leeman could only recollect fragments: conversations with the photographer, with the editorial board of the paper, studied diaries and letters by the writer, maps, telephone conversations. A week earlier it had brought them to Marlborough School, that venerable institution where Sassoon had spent a part of his youth. There they had wandered in the gardens among the old school buildings in the company of an extremely elderly teacher who had once been a friend of Sassoon's and who knew of an old boy on whose estate foxes were hunted. He made a call in his study while Leeman stood beside him: 'Sir Thomas? I'd like to introduce a friend of mine from Holland, Mr Leeman, a writer researching an article on Sassoon.' That's how England worked. Things were different in Holland, where people tended to send their daughter out of the room and lock up the silver if they heard you were a writer. Here it opened doors, particularly if you were introduced by a tutor from a boarding school that everyone had attended.

When Sir Thomas raised his glass in the salon, Leeman noticed that his eyes were misty. 'I never met Sassoon,' the old gentleman said. 'That's something I've always been terribly sorry about. He wrote so beautifully about fox-hunting. About England, as it was, until after the war. I've hunted with all of the people in his books. I served in the same regiment, The Royal Welch Fusiliers, albeit a war later. But I was never fortunate enough to meet him.'

Later, when the horsemen had arrived, and the master stood on the lawn surrounded by his hounds, he introduced Leeman and his photographer to his game warden, who was to drive them behind the horses in the Land Rover. Sir Thomas no longer hunted; but in honour of the visit he was going to read Sassoon by the fire. To Leeman's amazement he quoted *Memoirs of a Fox-Hunting Man* from memory before they drove away in the wake of the loudly baying hounds and the horses: 'Memories within memories; those red and black and brown coated riders return to me now without any beckoning, bringing along with them the wintry smelling freshness of the woods and fields'.

Viewed from up here, no movement could be discerned near the house, except for a plume of smoke rising from one chimney; Sir

Thomas' fire perhaps. Because of the hedges the land resembled a maze, which you could look into from above. On the far left of Leeman's field of vision there was movement: miniature horsemen were nervously circling a patch of low brown bushes, their jackets were tens of red dots in the autumn sun. He could barely make out the hounds, though you could hear their excited howls above the master's tinny horn clearly.

'They've lost him,' the photographer said. He was standing on the tailboard of the Land Rover with his largest telephoto lens on his camera. The photographer was very young, but Leeman liked travelling with him; he prepared his share of their literary trips so painstakingly that it sometimes seemed as though he recognised details in writers' landscapes rather than actually see them for the first time. Perhaps good photographers also imbued what they recorded with the value of memories, because their images seemed to have the essence of things that have always existed.

'What did he say?' the game warden asked.

Leeman poked his head inside. 'He thinks they've lost him.'

The game warden laughed. 'They lost him a long time ago,' he said. He held his hand in front of his mouth because his remaining teeth had been taken out a couple of days earlier. He'd told them that he was meant to get his new dentures in a week. He was seventy-one, a tall, thin man with mocking eyes. He sat straight as a rod in the car, so that his cap almost touched the roof. 'They've got a new master. He's good with his hounds, but he still has a lot to learn about foxes.' Half an hour earlier, with a grin on his face, he'd sent the Land Rover off in another direction, up into the hills while the master and the hounds descended to the stream. 'It's a crafty old fox he's trying to catch. He thinks it's fled under those bushes there. But I know for certain that it's crossed over Sir Thomas' land and it'll soon be coming this way over Mr Appleby's meadow.' He traced the fox's route on the windshield with his gloved finger.

The photographer clambered down off the tailboard and crossed to the corner of the field, where two of the hedges converged.

'Sassoon,' the game warden said. 'I've only read the book he wrote about fox-hunting. That's a very beautiful book.'

For the last two weeks Leeman had repeatedly been astonished to come across people who had read the writer's books. A man at the edge of a cricket pitch in Sassoon's home village, saying indignantly that of course he'd read Sassoon's books. 'He was born here, wasn't he? The man played cricket here. That's what he wrote about.' And Sir Thomas, who could quote passages from memory. This old game warden. Which old man, sitting on a bench at the edge of the Museumplein in Amsterdam, would know that the poet Herman Gorter had once played cricket there?

'It's all changed,' the man said. 'The foxes are the same, but I wouldn't give a farthing for the people any more. I don't know what's happened to them. I must have grown too old.'

'People don't change all that much,' said Leeman.

'With respect I'll have to disagree. It used to be about something other than money. Courtesy. Ideals. The war put an end to all that. Or wealth did.'

Leeman looked at the photographer and tried to imagine what he was seeing through his lens. The late afternoon light falling on steaming horses, crimson jackets, the water in the stream.

'Now it's only about money,' the game warden said. 'They can't even sit a horse properly. They jump right through the hedges. After the hunt I have to visit all the farms and repair the hedges and wrecked fences. Or round up escaped cattle, because they can't even close a gate behind themselves politely. That's modern England.'

These are exactly the same stories my father tells, Leeman thought. Things used to be better. The world used to be a village you could oversee.

'People think it was all about the aristocracy,' the man said. 'The hunt and so forth. But a farmer might be the master of the hounds. A butcher, the captain of the cricket team. You can read it all in Sassoon. If a farm-lad owned a good horse and could ride, he was the prince of the hunt. And if the Prince of Wales were there that day, and the lad was better, the Prince of Wales would doff his hat to him. Now you have to pay through the nose for a place in the hunt. They travel here from Germany and America to ride in one of those smart red jackets. Did you notice that there were two of them sitting on their horses smoking on that woodland path down there at the bottom? Smoking on the hunt.'

'Doesn't Sir Thomas ride with them any more?' Leeman asked.

'Sir Thomas?' He exploded with laughter again, with his hand in front of his mouth. 'He hasn't got a penny these days. He's had to get rid of his horses. Those slick new boys from the city have all the money now. They buy up everything around here. We just drove past that lovely house at the back. A Luyten country house. It was in the same family for generations. Now it's been bought by a Labour MP. He has huge dogs patrolling the estate, and nobody's allowed on to it. Oh, England's damned to ruin. Write that in your paper. There was a time when you could go to Tunbridge Wells with friends for a drink, and you didn't even have to lock your car. Now you have to carry a knife, because they'll crack open your head for a pound.'

I feel content, Leeman thought in amazement. I don't dare say happy – but I'm content to be standing here listening to the griping of an old man and viewing this landscape. Being here now I know why I want to write about Sassoon. He really wasn't any great shakes as a writer, and he certainly used to harp on a bit. He didn't do much else than play a bit of cricket around here and hunt foxes and read away the better part of his youth. But when he went to the French front during the war, he grew so enraged when he saw how all the young English and German boys were being butchered that he wrote a couple of poems and an article against the war, something unheard of for someone of his class. He wanted to be summoned before a court martial so that he could make his anger known, but influential friends made sure he ended up in a sanatorium. And afterwards he spent the rest of his life in a run-down, forty-room country house and wrote. About the war, but increasingly about the idyllic England of his youth. Why does that man move me? Why am I touched by being here in his landscape? Because he got angry once in his life about something that really mattered?

'Take care now,' the game warden said. The photographer looked around and touched his finger to his lips. The baying of hounds and the master's horn seemed a long way off, as if they'd crossed the stream in search of the fox on the other side of the house, whilst suddenly the fox emerged from a hedge no more than five metres from the photographer and calmly began to traverse the field.

'Look at him,' the game warden said softly. 'We can keep on talking, he knows we're not dangerous. Hounds are dangerous. Take a look at him goddammit. He's a gent, isn't he?'

The fox slunk past them unhurriedly with its belly close to the ground. Its back, and its protruding tail, which bobbed throughout its stealthy passage, caught the sun, and its pelt gleamed with life. It's watching us, Leeman thought. He felt a relaxation in his muscles as if he'd like to walk the same way, feeling the earth press against his feet. It's an individual, he thought. A life watching us and filing us away in its mind, not afraid but cautious. We're creatures that cast long shadows in the grass, but we're not dangerous. I exist in the mind of a fox, together with a grumbling old Englishman and a young photographer.

The sound of horses and hounds grew ever louder and the fox began to trot to the hedge on the far side of the field. It looked around again before it crept beneath the hedge.

The game warden stepped out of the car and came towards Leeman. He laughed so hard that he forgot to put his hand in front of his mouth. 'Such arrogance,' he said. 'He's safe now. He's going on to that Labour chap's land. They can't hunt there; he's had barbed wire threaded through his hedges. In two years he'll have a plague of foxes on his land.' At that moment Leeman heard the camera click. The photographer had taken their photo; Leeman and the old man standing by the car in the dwindling light. The photographer came up to them.

'Did you see the way it *looked* at us?' he said. 'I didn't dare move. I felt as if...' He started to laugh. 'I felt as if it'd think I was stupid if I took its photo.'

'You can smoke now,' the game warden said. 'He won't be back.'

Leeman saw the riders scattered along the stream below in little groups, looking as if they'd abandoned the search for the fox. Their shadows in the grass were longer than they were – tall, fragile horses and riders, changing form with every movement. The master sat motionless on his horse in the middle of a meadow, ringed by the hounds that had now fallen silent.

'I reckon he'll be heading home,' said the game warden. 'It's getting too dark. They're expecting snow. A lot of these folk still have a long drive ahead of them.'

They were still standing alongside the car. The photographer had packed away his cameras and the game warden had taken out a pipe and filled it. Now and then he placed it between his lips gently. Then all three of them looked up as a horse's hooves clattered on the track close by. On the far side of the field a horseman appeared behind a gate in the hedge, close to where the fox had disappeared. He bent over to unlock it, shoved it open with his foot and rode straight across the field towards them.

'Oh Jesus, that chap,' the game warden said. 'He can't even jump a hedge. His father bought some land here in the area and had a house built. They're totally loaded. He doesn't do a thing, as far as I know, but he's married to the daughter of an earl. They're from Oxford.' He circled around the car and sat behind the steering wheel.

The horseman stopped a couple of metres away from Leeman and the photographer and raised his top hat with a gloved hand. 'Hello,' he said. His glance slid from Leeman to the photographer, chose Leeman and said: 'Are you the writer?'

England, Leeman thought. They can tell by their plummy accents which school they went to. They gawp at you through the hedges as you walk past, checking if you're a dangerous outsider. They sit at tables outside tents in Africa in their dinner jackets, all *Bridge on the River Kwai*. But they still managed to find the time to create that working class with bad teeth and pasty faces that you see sat in the pubs. I think they've probably got special factories where they make the dismal clothes that these people wear, unpardonable bottle green and blue Terlenka trousers. But this one's bought his boots and red jacket at just the right tailor's in London, because it's not only by your accent they judge you, but by the cut of your coat and tie as well. You don't exist to them, but when their old teacher phones them up from that private school where they all bedded down together in little dormitories, then suddenly they know who you are a hundred miles away.

The photographer had distanced himself a few paces and was leaning against the car. 'He wants to be in the photo in the paper,' the game warden muttered.

'Yes,' said Leeman.

'It's marvellous that you're writing about Sassoon,' the horseman said. 'He wrote beautifully about fox hunting. The magic of it. Sassoon, I mean. But things have changed now, of course.'

The horseman was young, around thirty-five, Leeman guessed. He had dark hair, which curled out from beneath his hat, and a rather fat, dissatisfied face. He tapped his riding crop continually against his white chamois jodhpurs in impatience. His boots were perfect. Leeman was irritated that he had to look up at him like this.

'I suppose so,' he said.

'From Holland,' the horseman said. 'I go hunting in Holland quite often, actually.'

'Is that so?' Leeman said.

'What a twit,' the photographer muttered behind him. He climbed onto the running-board of the Land Rover and sat down next to the game warden. Leeman could hear them sniggering.

'Between the rivers,' the horseman said. 'The Betuwe. Do you know that part of the world?' His Oxford-English distorted the name of the place, but Leeman could picture it immediately: the little castle behind the dike, nestled among the orchards, his father's hand pointing out the driveways as they cycled past in the summer holidays.

'A friend of mine owns a castle there,' the horseman said in Dutch. 'He's a baron. That's a title we don't have here. Perhaps you know him?'

Leeman's grandfather was a switchman on the railway. In the mist one winter night he slipped on the icy rails at the local station and was run over by a shunting-engine. During Leeman's childhood holidays aunts used to take a little box out of a drawer lined with green velvet, which contained a fat silver pocket-watch with no glass and a silver coin folded almost double, which his grandfather had had in his pocket. Leeman's father was fourteen at the time of the accident and he had been forced to leave school to earn a living. He was apprenticed to an uncle who was a tailor. This was at the end of the First World War when Sassoon was being taken to a sanatorium by his dear friends.

On one particular day, Leeman's father was walking from the

town to the village where the baron's castle stood. He had a black valise over his arm containing a suit that the baron was to try on. It was an hour's walk. He took the gravel path behind the river-dike and cut across the big orchard behind the castle. He couldn't understand why the baron didn't come to fit his clothes at the tailor's like other customers, especially as the baron was the only one who had owned a car for many years, the first car that Leeman's father had ever seen. It had been raining and the grass in the orchard was sodden, so his trousers were soaked to the knee when he arrived at the castle. He walked through the front gate and up the drive. Two huge dogs ran up to him snarling. He didn't dare kick out at them because he was afraid they'd go for him and damage the suit, which his uncle had been working on for ten days. Then an old man in a black suit opened the huge door at the top of the steps a little and called off the dogs.

'What do you want?' the man asked.

'I've brought the suit from the tailor's,' Leeman's father said.

'Around the back,' the man snapped. He let the dogs in and shut the door firmly.

Leeman's father walked down the steps again and circled around the castle. He was angry because he'd been afraid of the dogs and had let himself be sent away by this man. He was still too young to know whether he wanted to be a socialist like his father who'd taken part in the railway strike of 1903; and he was still too young to know that he'd never step aside for anyone in his whole life. He knew he didn't want to be a tailor, and that he'd like to go to Indonesia at some stage. He was angry with life because his father had been cut in two by a train and his whole world had been transformed, and because his trousers were soaked and his arm was half numb from carrying the suit. This, in any case was how Leeman later pieced the story together from the scraps that his father, mother and stunned aunties had told him.

At the rear of the castle there were three steps leading down to a little door. Leeman's father knocked on it and was let in by a fat woman in a black dress with a white apron. Behind the door there was an enormous kitchen where a girl was standing at a stove dressed the same way as the older woman, but with a petite white bonnet on too.

Right behind Leeman's father the door opened again. A burly man entered with a rifle under his arm, a green hat on with a feather in it and big muddy boots. This was the baron.

'Who's that?' the baron asked the woman.

Leeman's father said he'd come from the tailor's to let him try the suit on. The baron sat down at the kitchen table, laid the rifle on the table and stuck out a muddy boot towards Leeman's father. He had a fat, reddish face and a moustache that curled upwards. Because he had no idea what the man meant, Leeman's father continued to stand where he was, with the suit folded over his arm.

'Pull my boots off, tailor,' the baron said.

'What?' Leeman's father said. The woman let out a gasp behind him. She grabbed the suit off his arm and gave him a shove.

'My boots,' the man said.

'I'm not your servant,' Leeman's father replied. He took the suit from the woman and walked out of the kitchen, back around the castle and down the drive. When he looked around at the gate, he could see that the baron, the old man and the woman in the white apron were watching him from the steps. He returned the suit to his uncle and went home. He was later apprenticed to another uncle, a watchmaker.

He never got to go to Indonesia because his mother couldn't bear the disgrace. When he met Leeman's mother he was a professional watchmaker. Her father had a gardening firm and maintained the gardens at the castle. Her mother went to the castle once a week to collect the fine wash, which was done in the large scullery at the nursery. Leeman's mother's engagement to the young watchmaker was probably her only act of defiance in her whole life; her parents saw no future in her association with a boy who was not of the middle classes, but she was determined to have her way.

One Saturday evening, Leeman's father went to collect his fiancée for a stroll. It was summertime, and he was wearing a light new suit, with two-tone summer shoes and a straw boater. He was a young craftsman, and he didn't step aside for anyone. When he walked into the scullery at the nursery his intended was ironing the baron's shirts. Her mother was scrubbing down the sink and her father was sitting at the table reading the paper with his cap on, exactly as Leeman would always see him later.

'Aren't you finished yet?' Leeman's father asked.

'She has to finish the ironing first,' his intended mother-in-law said.

'My fiancée doesn't do ironing when we're going out,' Leeman's father said. 'And certainly not for that bastard.' He put the iron on the stove and said to Leeman's mother: 'get dressed'.

Her father put down his paper and said: 'She's going to finish her work first. Who do you think you are, with all your bolshy chat.'

Leeman's father grabbed the tray and the tea-set off the table and flung it at the gardener's head, took his bride by the arm and yanked her outside. There, on the gravel path beside the city walls, a street photographer took their photo: Leeman's father with his arrogant boyish face beneath his straw hat; Leeman's petite mother with her Charleston dress and her broad flowery bonnet, gazing up fearfully, but in love, at the man whose anger she would allay her whole life with patience and geniality and fine meals. Leeman had been given the photo by his mother years earlier when she was cleaning out some cupboards. 'Engaged, 1930' was written on the back. They looked like figures out of a story by Scott Fitzgerald. A year later the town had grown too claustrophobic for Leeman's father and they were married and moved to Amsterdam.

'My wife's a friend of that princess of yours,' the horseman said. 'The wild one, who's divorced and so on. She knows the baron, that's why we hunt there. Is she still having an affair with that journalist? You probably know him. Writers, journalists. They all know one another.'

Leeman looked at the horseman's boots. They were caked with mud from the fruitless hunt after the fox. How does one discover who one is, he thought. Everything's chance, isn't it? I wouldn't be standing here now if my father had carried on living there. Would he understand if I tried to explain how there's a long, invisible thread running through time, from the moment that he shut the kitchen door behind him to the place I'm standing now, where the life inside a fox just looked at me?

The horseman stretched out on his mount so that one muddy boot pointed towards Leeman. Leeman stared intently at the belly in the tight red jacket, the self-satisfied thighs, stretching the rough fabric of the white jodhpurs, the contorted face.

'A funny lot, you writers,' the horseman said.

'What?' said Leeman.

'Sassoon too. He wrote a lovely book, but he was quite mad, wasn't he? Bit of a pacifist.'

Leeman felt a strange anger welling up inside him, which actually had nothing to do with what the man had said, but perhaps had more to do with the fact that he was obliged to look up at him. At the same time he had the feeling that he might burst out laughing at any second. Down in the valley below the master's horn blew for the end of the hunt. The horseman looked down on him questioningly.

'Drop dead,' Leeman said in Dutch and walked over to the Land Rover and stepped in. The game warden and the photographer were sitting there quaking with laughter. The game warden started the engine and drove off. The horseman raised his hat as they drove by.

'You looked as if you might eat him, horse and all,' the game warden said.

'Why did you get so angry?' the photographer asked. 'I couldn't hear what he was saying, but I know that face of yours.'

Leeman lit a cigarette. They bumped down a steep muddy path towards the valley. A light was burning behind one of the windows at the house.

'Perhaps it was his boots,' Leeman said.

Breaking the Silence

Bernlef

translated by PC Evans

On the 29th of September 199* the popular uprising erupted, which a year later would culminate in the dissolution of the state. The then seventy-year-old poet H remembered it thus: 'True to habit I turned on the television at 7.30 in the evening to watch the sports programme. Instead I saw an excitable assembly of poorly dressed men sat at a prop-up table, the majority of whom were no more than thirty. An older man with horn-rimmed spectacles and a mobile black moustache was doing most of the talking. He was holding forth on the abolition of the existing order. Undoubtedly this was some documentary drama or other about a South American country where imperialism was on the verge of being replaced by real manifest socialism. I switched to the second channel. There I saw the same group. Behind the table, people were walking in and out of shot waving papers excitedly. The composition of the group at the table continually changed. No one appeared to be in charge. Only then did it start to become clear to me. They said that the population had crossed the borders of the neighbouring countries *en masse*. In the capital people had started demolishing the wall that divided the city in two. My whole body began to tremble. My first thought? If only Marit had been here to see this.'

Twenty years ago H had been condemned to silence. He was expelled from the Writers Union and exiled to the hamlet of V, where he lived in an old farmhouse near the lake with his wife Marit. His collections *Cellar Songs* (1968) and *At Room Strength* (1971) had sold out within a day of publication and had been banned shortly after. His name had disappeared from the hand-books, the newspapers and the magazines. But over the years his poems had multiplied and spread throughout the country as innu-merable re-typed copies. Some of his lines such as "I stayed so that I could go/I went so that I could stay" and "I no longer loved this country/I was the only one who could see/that this country does not exist" had become almost mythical. The authorities had driven him further and further into isolation. He was constantly monitored by the police from the General Surveillance Department; his letters were opened or withheld, his telephone tapped. The police regularly barged into his house to confiscate his manuscripts. But they never found anything. I don't write poetry any more, he replied to their questioning. But they didn't believe him, of course. They kept tabs on him. He no longer wrote, but his silence became legendary; the western press even referred to it as deafening. On several occasions he was invited to come and read there. But of course each time he was refused a visa. When his silence continued to grow, someone from the government came to visit him and offered him an exit visa. H knew what that meant. He refused and said: 'It's not that I'm keeping silent, it's just that I can't speak any more.' When, in October 199*, his wife drowned in the lake (she was extremely myopic and there was a thick mist that evening) H seemed to be in every respect a broken man. We don't have a thing to fear from him now, the chief of the GSD intimated to the head of state. But H's silence became more and more talked about, and the subject of scores of clandestinely distributed poems. His refusal to write stirred the writing in others. On scores of issues people asked them-selves: what would H have said about this? The GSD was powerless. How were they meant to react to this emptiness, this absence of words, this endless and unremitting silence? Control of his move-ments was tightened. But nothing in any way suggested a danger to the state. Even the inhabitants of V were unable to say anything

about him. He came to pick up his groceries at the shop twice a
week. The police scrutinised his shopping lists, but couldn't find
anything suspect in them. They spied on him with binoculars when
he rowed his boat out onto the lake and moored up at one of the
little islands. He'd sit there for hours under an oak tree staring out
over the water. The police asked themselves what he was thinking.
Not even his lips moved. They wrote in their reports that H had
spent his day in prayer so that they were at least able to come home
with something. In one report, one of the officers even compared
him to a statue. Ultimately, his presence alone was subversive.
Maybe the head of government had momentarily pondered having
him liquidated, but had abandoned the idea. Instead, it was decided
to grant him rehabilitation. This he refused, of course.

H's silence was broken on the twenty-ninth of September 199*. He
was one of the first writers to appear on TV. With his sagging jowls
and the bags beneath his eyes, H looked like an old dog, a bulldog.
He compared language to a piece of land in the wake of a deluge;
everything covered with a thick layer of sludge. 'Only when we have
purified our language of thirty years of deceit, suspicion and
cowardice can we again write without having to be ashamed.' At the
close of the broadcast he looked straight into the camera. 'Twenty
years of house arrest have caused me to forget the world outside. On
the other hand, I've come to know my own house extremely well.' He
said this without a trace of irony or bitterness. In response to the
question of whether he would take up the pen again, he only smiled.

He now had to get used to the postman coming every day with a
great amount of post and papers. Letters from admirers and admir-
eresses, invitations to come to give talks, or to read his poems
somewhere. The mountain of post on his desk grew. He didn't
answer a single letter; it was as if he considered his handwriting too
precious for use. In reality he had grown so attached to his silence
that he didn't want to relinquish it. If the telephone rang he had his
stock response ready. 'That is a subject of which I have no understanding.' The spy from the GSD, who had stood picket in his
mouse-grey car up near the burned out windmill, had disappeared.

Still H did not alter the pattern of his life. Twice a week he visited the country shop, where the family R served him with respect and a degree of apprehension. Ultimately, everyone had betrayed everyone else. The old distrust still hadn't softened. So the jokes made about the defunct regime in the shop were circumspect and uttered furtively. It turned out that the president had owned a luxurious palace by the coast. They'd seen photos of it in the paper. An example of real manifest socialism. They discussed the pros and cons of emigration. H was no longer asked his opinion of anything.

In the newspapers and on the television, meanwhile, the knives were being sharpened. Filled with repugnance, H saw how everyone was rapidly trying to set their house in order. Just like after the big war, it suddenly turned out that everyone had actually been a hero, or at least had intended to be. Only G stood firm. He kept referring to himself as a communist. H had a certain amount of respect for him. This was one person at least who didn't start turning the moment that the wind blew from a different direction. But he couldn't conceal the fact that he pondered G's future with malicious delight. It would be the definitive end for his fist-thick novels of peasant life, his panegyric for a teaching, in which real life constantly had to be postponed until various enemies of the people were eliminated first. For years, G had been the chairman of the Writers Union and was thus directly responsible for H's expulsion. Now he would be the first to be thrown out of the new union. Everyone had modified their position, but the methods remained the same. The handful of exiled dissidents returned to great acclamation. They were the lions now, while S, for example, who had sometimes struck a compromise with the censor, could have had them all as a writer. There was freedom of expression, but the literature was still as politicised as during the regime. Under these circumstances there was no point in taking a side. H continued to be silent, though his silence was no longer seen as an act of resistance, but as a refusal to participate in the new order. Yes, that's how his colleagues referred to it: the new order.

H lived off the modest pension, which they hadn't dared to take away from him. Each day he took his usual walk through the woods or rowed the boat out to the island, where he would stare out over the rippling water from beneath the oak tree. If he were ever to write anything again, it would have to be about her, about Marit. She had poor eyesight. On that particular evening she must have wandered through the mist and stumbled into the water by accident. He would not consider any other possibility. It was October; she must have been overcome by the cold. They only found her body after three days of dragging the lake. They took it to the hospital in the provincial capital B. It was only then that he was informed. Later they sent him a copy of the police report. A precise list of everything that they had brought up while dragging. A tractor, model Ferz, assembly year 1931, six wooden cartwheels, two flatboats, a scythe, fourteen separate planks from a ruined jetty, three hawsers, two fishing-nets, and a rusted money box, which was empty. She was listed sixteenth. After reading the report he tore it up immediately. The funeral took place in silence. No one from V came. He was left standing there alone with that one deep red rose clutched in his fist. It was only after three days that he picked up the phone and called a few friends. That was four years ago, but he still missed her and admonished himself for how little of her he could remember. Sometimes in the mornings when waking up he imagined that he could hear her voice. Or no, not her voice, but an interior echo of it. They had been together for twenty-seven years. I took life with her for granted he considered. That's what he thought now, now that it was too late.

On the outside then he might look like a statue, a dead-straight old man with grey hair stuck up in a bristling quiff, as though electrified, but on the inside a chaos of opposing currents reigned. He considered his life with Marit to have been a chain of missed opportunities. I didn't take enough account of the possibility of her death, he told himself, I let too much pass me by. And there beneath the oak tree, staring out at the lake water, he tried to visualise her gestures, her way of walking, or tripping rather, her shortsighted pottering. But he could see nothing. His proud silence gave way to an overwhelming feeling of shame. He grieved for her disappearance, which seemed to him to be more definite with each passing day. Photos seemed strange to him; this wasn't the wife that he had been searching for. Wasn't she concealed inside him anywhere? He tried to draw the objects in his house to his aid; he pressed the piano keys to conjure up her short, strong fingers, her inarticulate humming as she played Chopin's mazurka in C sharp minor third, much too slowly, her reading glasses balanced on the tip of her nose, squinting at the score on the music stand in front of her. But even the objects in the house had let her go. Dust and dirt advanced from the corners of the room. Even stains had become dear to him now. They proved that the two of them had once lived there together. The desire to write had become entirely alien to him. A friend had sent him Eugenio Montale's sequence of poems about his dead wife, 'Xenia'.

> Sweet little insect,
> For some reason or other named fly,
> This evening while reading Deuteronomy-Isaiah
> In the approaching darkness
> You suddenly appeared beside me,
> But without spectacles,
> So you couldn't see me
> And I couldn't see you
> Without your lenses' gleam.

The poems moved him deeply, but at the same time they were the irrefutable proof that an end had come to his writing. All art was surrogate for life. 'When I used to write poems' was a phrase he used more and more often now. If the police from the GSD were still checking his shopping lists they would see that he consumed increasing quantities of red wine. A young Norwegian posted him a thesis on his poetry. The extracts quoted seemed as though they had been written by someone else, someone that he'd left behind. He wrote back that he wouldn't be able to meet her. The woods surrounding his house seemed to draw him. As if, through his years of silence, he had crossed the border and become a tree himself, one of them. He longed for death, the one thing that would release him from this gnawing absence. I want to follow Marit. But the thought of wading into the lake daunted him. When he rowed out to the island and stuck his hand into the water for a second, he was stunned by the fierce cold that almost seemed to burn his hand. He peered at the dripping fingers that he had withdrawn from the dark

water with lightning speed. Besides himself, there was also a body.
And that didn't want to die.

The day that G came to visit the sun shone. The fringes of the
chestnut leaves displayed their familiar rusty brocade. Everywhere
chestnuts that had burst out of their husks lay glimmering in the
grass with the sheen of polished furniture. G drove his old light-blue
Skoda up to his door. Standing at the window H saw him step out,
hesitantly, and take a look around, as if still frightened of being
followed. Since the revolution, though, everyone had kept to themselves. The tattletales were once again posing as real citizens. H
estimated that they must total about seventy per cent of the population. And as for the past, however recent, not a word was spoken.

G was still tall and slender. His straight hair had greyed at the
temples. H had sometimes thought that his long pointy nose and
small lips gave him the aspect of a bird, a sparrow hawk. Now he
simply said to G to come in.

'You can't just stand there,' he said.

G nodded, stepped into the hall and waited until H had closed
the door behind him.

'I've come to talk to you,' he said. 'If you want me to at least.'

H was irritated by the timid, submissive tone.

'Of course,' he said. 'Why not? I don't get that many people here.'

They went into the living room, which looked out onto the
wood's edge, the room with the black piano, with its lid shut.

'I didn't know you played piano,' said G to start somewhere.

'Marit played.'

G was silent. With a sweep of his hand H directed him to a chair
by the table and then sat opposite him. He placed his hands
together and studied the nicotine-stained yellow fingernails of his
left hand.

G blinked, his right hand reached for the support of the table's
edge. His black blazer was too big for him. He looked tired. He
pressed his fingertips together, bent forwards towards H slightly
and said: 'It's over'.

H nodded. 'Everyone has their time,' he said. 'But at least you
can write what you want now.'

G shook his head slowly. 'It's over,' he repeated. 'Nobody'll publish me now.'

'Surely you haven't come to complain,' H said sharply.

G was stunned. No, on the contrary, he had come to make his apologies. He should never have agreed to the demands of the authorities to have H thrown out of the Writers Union.

'Old business,' said H. 'Now it's your turn.'

H knew that the newly convened Writers Union was engaged in a purge, and he hadn't wanted to join because, as he informed them in his letter, 'he no longer wrote'.

G felt driven into a corner. It wouldn't have surprised H if there were soon tears in his eyes. He got up to bring a bottle of red wine.

'Let's have a drink first,' he said.

'To what, asked G absently.

'To the revolution, of course,' said H.

'To the comeback,' said G.

That's how H preferred to hear him. 'Sure, you can look at it like that too,' he said.

'Do you really believe in it then, in the revolution,' said G.

'I'm too old for all that,' said H.

G was more than twenty years his junior. When G had become the chairman of the Writers Union, he was an ambitious young novelist who went around in jeans and a gleaming black leather jacket. His voice had sounded firm and clear then, assured of his rightness. He'd also worn a martial moustache.

'Did you really believe in what you wrote,' H asked. 'In those novels full of undulating grain, in those five-year plans, which were always achieved in the nick of time, in the final chapter.'

'They had an exemplary function,' said G. 'That's how it should have been.'

'But that's not how it was,' said H and smiled as he filled their glasses.

'I should really boot you out of the door,' he said, 'but I'm interested in how you were able to lie to yourself all that time.'

'They weren't lies,' said G, 'they were prognoses for the future. A believer can wait a long time for a miracle.'

'And now the miracle has come to pass,' said H.

'That's still to be seen,' said G. People will start to feel homesick for the old order, you'll see.'

H sighed. 'I don't want any order any more', he said. 'I just want to die.'

G shook his head contemptuously. He was a communist. In the name of that system people had been murdered in their hundreds of thousands, but a communist did not believe in death. He did, however, believe in necessary sacrifice, offered up on the altar of history.

G stood and walked over to the window with his hands in his pockets. H looked at his back and was astonished by his absence of hate.

'I've looked into my file,' said G. 'The GSD was even more efficient than I'd imagined.'

'In what way?' said H. 'I take it you were working for them.'

'It was unavoidable,' said G. 'But when I read my file I found that I was under surveillance too.'

G turned around and walked back to his chair. His face was hunting for an expression, but couldn't find a fitting one quickly enough. A man in panic.

'I asked to see my file so that I could defend myself later,' he said.

'Maybe there'll be no trial,' said H. 'People have other things to be concerned about. By the way, they say that seventy per cent of the population was working for the GSD. There's just nowhere to make a start.'

'That must certainly be true judging by all those cellars filled with files,' said G. 'Why don't you go and take a look. You have that right now.'

'And find what,' said H. 'I haven't done a thing this whole time but keep silent.'

'I can hardly believe it,' said G. 'Surely you must have some things in your desk.'

H shook his head. 'You robbed me of my language,' said H. 'I wouldn't have thought it possible, but it was.'

H pointed to a daddy-long-legs in a corner of the room, with its long legs groping towards the ceiling.

'In a little while it'll fall and then start crawling forwards again.

A person can get by very well without literature.'

G seemed to be lost in his thoughts for a moment. Then he said: 'You have no idea of everything that the GSD knows about you'. 'The tiniest things. Things that you've totally forgotten. They didn't discriminate. Everything was written down.'

'We have always been a country of compulsive accountants,' said H. 'It comes from our lack of self-confidence. We've never really believed in this country. It was only when something was written in a report that it actually seemed real to us.'

G stood up and thrust out his hand. 'You understand how ashamed I am,' he said. 'I realise, of course, that it is essentially unforgivable.'

'If I were someone else, I'd shoot you down right here,' said H. 'As long as you know that.'

When H went to the capital and reported at the office of the former GSD, which was still hidden behind a copper name-plate bearing the letters 'Profile AB – Import and Export', he was promptly admitted to the director, a young man with light-blue eyes, a springy step and a somewhat overly-enthusiastic handshake. P.

'You have to understand that I've only recently been appointed,' he said. 'The cellars are still quite a labyrinth to me too.'

'Are there many people who want to see their files,' asked H.

'At first there was a quite a stampede. But now the novelty's worn off...'

'The novelty?' asked H.

'Whether or not your neighbour worked for the department, or who was blabbing about you at work.'

'And then?'

'Nothing really. There's simply nowhere to begin.'

'So you also think that everything should be forgotten?' asked H.

'That would be best,' said the young man. 'The shame is just too great.'

He led H down to the cellars. The young director's grey polyester trousers were a little too short. H gripped the banister on the stairs. When they came to a halt before a steel-lined door and P held it open for him, he said: 'There are a couple of members of staff wandering around who can help you further. You'll recognise them by their grey overalls. If you need anything else, you know where my office is.'

H heard the young man sprinting up the stairs two at a time, as if he were on the run from something. H recognised the smell of densely packed, slowly mouldering paper: the university library of J, where he had once studied. His eyes had to adjust to the scant light in the cellar, which penetrated through a series of little latticed panes. Every now and then he saw men's and women's legs walking by outside. In front of him there were rows of iron shelves, bursting out on both sides with files stuffed into brown folders, apparently stretching into infinity. He shuffled slowly along the head of the aisles without venturing into the labyrinth.

In the distance he could see one of the members of staff standing behind a trolley in the grey overalls described by P. There was nobody else to be seen in this immense cellar. A clammy silence pervaded, which was only occasionally disturbed by sounds from outside. The man in the overalls saw him coming from a distance. H introduced himself. 'I've had permission from the director to look into my file.' The slightly older man nodded. He had a grey complexion, as if his face were covered with a fine layer of powder. The dark trace of a scar ran across his left cheek. The man shuffled ahead of him in unlaced soldier's boots. H noticed that he had a slight limp. He breathed heavily.

'We have to go to section c,' the man said without looking around. 'That's where the files are that are concerned with literature.'

H had only told the man his name, but the official had evidently been informed who he was.

The space that they now entered was lit by a row of neon tubes on the ceiling. The man came to a halt in front of one of the stacks of shelves. He counted the spines of the files.

'Twenty-one,' he said. 'You were important. Do you want to look at them all?'

'Let's start with the first one,' said H. 'Then we'll see how it goes.'

The official took a fat brown folder down off the shelf and walked over to a worn-out table surrounded by some kitchen chairs. He placed the folder on the table and pointed to one of the chairs by way of invitation.

'On the right-hand side of the table there's a little buzzer,' he said. 'If you need to know anything just press it.'

H sat with his closed file in front of him. His heart beat. He could hear the officials shuffling in the distance. He opened the folder.

The file began on the 27th of September 197★ with the report of the editorial meeting of *New Roads*, where he had tendered his resignation as editor-in-chief. One of the editorial staff present must have compiled the report. L or R or maybe even the diminutive, asthmatic V? His arguments had been recorded correctly. 'I can no longer perform credibly as editor-in-chief if decisions about editorial policy are taken at the Ministry of Culture.'

H browsed further. Over the course of two hours he saw his whole life at that time pass by. It was only now that he was studying one document after another that he realised with how much deliberation his isolation was effected.

When he'd finished the first file, he got up and fetched the next. He didn't need the official for this. During the course of the day he witnessed the treachery of his friends. The first house search May 22nd 198★. A list of the confiscated manuscripts and books, written in a schooled, laboured style. He could see the man standing in front of him again, the way he sat at his kitchen table meticulously itemising the manuscripts, which two others had rifled from drawers and desks, the tip of his furred tongue poking through his teeth. Titles of poems, which he still vaguely remembered, an article about the chromatic theories of Goethe and Wittgenstein, the synopsis of a film that had never been made. At the bottom of the page, next to the date, was the signature of the squinty man from the GSD, ending in an elegant flourish, as though he were relieved that a chore had been dispensed with. Marit had left the house in a rage. A fact that hadn't been noted anywhere. She trailed through the house after those two plain-clothes policemen like a watchdog. She demanded a list of the papers and books confiscated and when the squinty man refused she stormed off into the woods in fury. And he? He had been numb with fear. He hadn't obstructed them in any way. He leafed further nervously. The confiscated manuscripts were not in the file. Perhaps they were elsewhere. Or they had been destroyed by the GSD. He leaned back in his chair. His eyes were burning. It made no difference now. The GSD had made sure that he had been driven into oblivion, even when he was still alive. Suddenly, he was too tired to continue. He pressed the buzzer.

The man in the overalls nodded with understanding.

'It's too much for most people,' he said. 'Do you want to come back another time?'

H nodded. 'Tomorrow,' he said.

'I'll leave everything where it is then.'

H spent the night in a hotel. He lay in the bath for a long time and then fell into a deep and dreamless sleep. When he awoke the next morning he felt as though he had worked the whole night.

On his way to the Avenue of Triumph, where the building was situated that housed the GSD archive, H remarked how run-down the houses looked. This was the fruit of years of artificial rent control ('an affordable home for one and all'), a policy which resulted in not a cent remaining for maintenance. Peeling window frames, crooked runners, unpainted, battered doors. And everywhere the reek of oil and coal. The people he passed lived in a free country, but they looked as though they bore a heavy burden. Free but unemployed.

At a street corner there was a flat cart parked on the pavement. On the cart there was a black piano, with a pug-nosed man in fingerless gloves playing a melody that he recognised, but couldn't put a name to. The man had turned up the collar of his jacket and every now and then he blew on his fingers between two passages. H carried on walking.

At the archive the porter eyed him distrustfully and then picked up the telephone. He was one of the old guard. No admittance without identity papers and a special permit. Following the telephone call, however, he was allowed to continue. 'I know the way,' he said.

The cellar was deserted. It was still early. In section c the files that he had read the day before lay undisturbed on the table. He walked over to one of the aisles and stood in front of the rows of bulging folders for quite some time. What was the sense of doing this? Wasn't it just masochism, to rake up these twenty lost years by sifting through reports, notations, the eyewitness reports of spies who had kept watch on his house for years from their cars with binoculars? His hand moved down the line of brown folders hesitantly, and then removed one. He went to the table with the folder and sat down.

The file began on the 24th of October 198*. The first page had been composed on a typewriter with a worn-out ribbon. The faint letters seemed as though they'd like to withdraw from beneath his gaze. His lips moved as he read the text. He had to swallow hard a couple of times.

> M: Don't keep putting that same shirt on all the time.
> H: As long as I don't stink…
> M: That won't take much longer.
> H: Is there any coffee left?
> M: On the stove.

According to the reporter, this conservation took place at 9.23 in the morning. It was incredible. They must have installed a hidden microphone during one of the house searches. And somewhere, at another location, someone had sat and typed out the entire tape. Hundreds of pages of it.

November 6th, 11.15 am.

> H: Has the squirrel passed by yet?
> M: No, I haven't seen Vicky today.
> H: That fat-ball in the apple tree's almost gone, do you see?
> M: I'll buy a new one this afternoon. Then the titmice'll come back.

Vicky. That's what Marit had called the squirrel, with its little nervous rotating head and the thin tail that showed that it must already be quite old. Vicky, after an old aunt who had a phobia for dirt and germs and couldn't sit still for a second.

Everything that they'd said to each other in the living room all those years was noted down here. All those daily conversations about nothing in particular, which demonstrated how closely the older couple had grown together. A ritual of reassurances, half-uttered sentences, innuendos and good-humoured complaints.

February 2nd 198★

> M: Can I throw this paper away?
> H: Let me see. It's a first draft.
> (Someone had drawn a question mark in the margin here with a pencil.)
> M: I'd hold on to it then if I were you.
> H: I never go back to earlier drafts.

H remembered what this was all about. In January 198★ he had begun translating the poems of Catullus. For pleasure; to keep himself busy. He could see Marit standing there with the paper in her hand, dangling it by a corner, as though she were disgusted by it. Marit didn't like Catullus. She found his poems obscene. It keeps the naughty boy alive inside me, he had told her. Besides it was a good opportunity to brush up on his Latin.

He stared at the grey-distempered cellar walls. There she was again, with a wry little laugh as she called him an old pervert, tripping closer in stockinged feet and standing on her toes to kiss him on the forehead. We collect wrinkles the way Vicky does beechnuts, he had said to her once. Her face, even when old, had seemed to him to be so indestructible.

Something was underlined here. <u>Piano music</u>. The writer hadn't recognised the piece and to be on the safe side had placed a question mark after the words. He tried to imagine the man or woman who had sat there diligently typing out these conversations day after day. Did they really think that they could uncover secrets like this, which they could use to blackmail him later? He and Marit didn't have any secrets from each other and they rarely talked about politics. Over the years they had begun to act as though they were living in a different country. This country does not exist, he had once written, and meanwhile, nobody had realised how literally he had meant it.

However unremarkable their conversations often might have been, now that he was re-reading them they filled his mind with images. Nodding and laughing with recognition, he worked his way through the files. At that moment, the conversations were more dear to him than any masterpiece could have been. In all their commonness they opened the portals of his memory.

He extended his stay at the hotel by a week. In the evenings he went in search of busy restaurants and cafes. He felt part of life again and realised that he owed this happiness to the police officers of the GSD. In the mornings, he woke with a boyish excitement. He sang in the shower and wrung his hands with contentment. Everything had been preserved. Thanks to the state spies not one word of his life with her had been lost.

On the seventh day of his visit the director came to look him up.

'You are making quite a job of it,' said P in a friendly manner, as he sat down on the corner of the table. 'Are you going to write a book about it?'

H smiled and then looked at him in earnestness.

'I'm seeing everything again as if it were new,' he said.

'Aren't you shocked by everything that you've been reading?' asked P.

'You can't begin to imagine how happy I am,' said H.

'There's been talk that our country is going to be united with one of our neighbours. That we'll cease to exist as an independent nation,' said the director.

'This archive's worth it's weight in gold,' said H and pointed to the rows of shelves around him with one hand.

'They were crazy at the GSD,' answered P, thinking that H meant everything he said ironically.

'Of course they were,' said H. 'Fortunately. This should never be lost.'

'For historical reasons you mean,' P enquired.

H nodded. 'The life in a country has never been so exhaustively documented.' He turned over a page and read out loud:

M: The tiles around the cooker are starting to get loose.
H: I'll see if I can find some glue somewhere. Perhaps R sells glue.
I have to go to the shop later anyway.
M: Don't forget then.
H: I never forget a thing.

The director shook his head.

'All that inanity,' he said, 'all of that information that is of absolutely no importance. To anyone at all.'

'That's the heart of it,' H replied, and closed the folder in front of him. 'And what about the tapes?'

P repeated H's question.

'The tapes that all these conversations were recorded on.'

P shrugged his shoulders.

'They still used those big reel to reels then. Tapes were expensive. They were used over and over.'

For a moment it looked as though H were about to faint. He turned white as chalk.

'When everything had been written down the tapes were erased,' P continued. 'As I said, they were crazy at the GSD.'

The director led him to the outside door. He watched the aged poet leave. Yes, he looked remarkably like a dog. The people that H met on the broad pavement looked at his wrinkled beaming face with astonishment. Nobody's forgotten him, thought the director with satisfaction as he turned back inside. After all this time everyone on the street still recognises him.

The next morning H heard on the radio that G had committed suicide. At once a melody ran through his mind. He began to hum softly. That pianist on the cart. Of course, it was the mazurka in c sharp minor third. She couldn't escape him any longer. He opened the marbled notebook on the table in front of him and began to write, at first slowly and unaccustomed, but then gradually quicker and quicker.

Moped on Sea

JMA Biesheuvel

translated by PC Evans

Isaac had been standing on the poop deck for hours. He was a pleasant, but slightly strange boy: when working on board he yearned for a job on land and when working in an office, he yearned for the sea. He couldn't bear the tedious monotony of life ashore and had no money to make sea voyages. However, when he was aboard ship – in the capacity of a random crew member (he wore glasses, so was always a cabin boy, mess hand or officer's valet, never a seaman let alone a helmsman, his great dream...) – he had to cope with the rough banter of the sailors, who played cards with their knives on the table and called one another and Isaac everything under the sun. Isaac never really fitted in. He fitted in least of all in a ship's company, even less than in the harbour, the bottling plant, the factory or the office, yet it was precisely on a ship that he always imagined he'd find true romance. When work was over you'd always find him standing on the poop deck. It was now two hours past midnight, but Isaac was still there because it was a moonlit night, and you could see all the familiar stars of the southern hemisphere and the dangerous, white, foaming propeller wash behind the ship (anyone who's stood on the poop deck of a sailing ship for hours will know that by night or at any ungodly hour during the day, in the rain or mist, in arctic regions or tropics, in grey, green or clear blue water ships always, but always, sail along a white road, this road runs from the horizon to the propeller, a drowning man crossing the path a quarter of an hour later would no longer see this road).

There was a delicious sultry wind. If you looked carefully you could actually see the horizon, or a little closer by the light of a ship tacking away, which, if Isaac had been an hour earlier, would have been sailing straight towards him. But, as will be demonstrated, the senses can deceive us. There are philosophers who maintain that anything that exists is imaginary and the antithesis cannot be proved! Isaac was sailing on a tramp steamer and he never saw any other ships at night. He considered how long it would take before he was home again. He looked at the winches, the bollards, the hawsers, the railing and the easy chair he'd placed on the poop deck for himself. And then at a given moment Isaac saw the light in the distance make an abrupt turn, it seemed to trace a narrow arc on the water and come straight towards him. When it continued to move closer Isaac concluded that it almost certainly couldn't represent, or be, a ship, given the degree it was susceptible to the rolling of the waves, and primarily because it remained as just one light. A ship with only its stern light on? Hazardous. When the peculiar vehicle approached to within two hundred fathoms of Isaac he could make out that it was a moped. For the first time in his life something had happened to Isaac that might 'rightly be described as remarkable'. What he now saw no one in their wildest dreams could dare, or even be able to conceive of. At first Isaac was afraid, but all in all he couldn't assume that a new prophet or Messiah would ferry himself across the globe in this manner. Although the Christians do indeed assert that Jesus walked on water. The moped now came to within sixteen metres of Isaac. He was calling out and waving frantically, but in all his excitement he forgot to cast out the rope ladder. This was brought to his attention by the moped's rider. It was clear from his accent that the stranger was a countryman of Isaac's. He steered his moped in a very remarkable and extremely careful manner towards the rope ladder, and while still seated on his moped, he drew himself up alongside the smooth hull of the ship like a boxer feeling out his opponent in the ring, his torso bobbing slightly, his feet dancing and making parrying or indeed aggressive movements with his arms, and then hoopla! he sprang onto the rope ladder in one motion, moped and all. 'Careful, careful,' he kept calling. The man was wearing glasses that were terribly misted up, and a cap with leather flaps that served to screen his eyes and ears from seawater, and which stuck out a long way. The moped was a normal moped. It had no special features. Isaac helped the man to haul his moped on deck. The man said: 'Give me something to eat.' Isaac went to fetch it. He remarked that the sailors and the helmsmen and the engine room crew had already gone off to their bunks. When Isaac returned he asked the stranger: 'Why do you ride on the water?' The man responded that he wanted to set a record.

'How is it possible for you to ride on the water?' Isaac asked in astonishment. 'It's merely a question of practice,' the man said, ' I began by laying a pin on the water. If you do that very carefully, it stays afloat. After a while, I tried heavier and heavier objects. It was quite natural for me to use my moped and eventually I took my first humble laps on the municipal pond. Now I ride all over the world. I never go ashore anywhere, but because I have to eat now and then, I often head to a ship. I prefer to go in the dead of night. When everyone's asleep. I went to the ships in broad daylight the first few times, but some people ended up going doolally. First they screamed that this was the best thing that had ever happened to them in their entire lives, and then they began talking gibberish or else they went mad. I'm planning on travelling forty thousand kilometres over the sea; a few kilometres more won't be a problem, as long as I've circumnavigated the entire globe. I want to do something that nobody else has managed before. That's always been my ideal.' 'Aren't you ever afraid of drowning?' Isaac asked.

'Oh no,' the man answered. 'It's the way you ride; that's the important thing, and always being careful when revving and throttling back of course. You should never take on a high wave with too much speed, for example, otherwise the tyre walls get wet, and once that's happened, there's just no end to it.' 'Yes, I understand,' said Isaac, who gazed at the man full of admiration. The man was sitting there truly eating his fill. And he drank copious quantities of milk

and alcohol. At last, he asked for a bottle of iodine, because this was
something he had need of. In the meantime, an hour had passed
and the man slung his moped back overboard and draped it from
the rope ladder. Then he took his leave of Isaac. He asked if it might
be possible for him to join for the rest of the journey on the moped,
as a driver's mate. 'Perhaps I could navigate or something, I have
sailed a lot,' he ended his request. But the man burst out laughing.
'You'd have to train for years first,' the man said, but if I really
wanted to *per se*, I'd take you with me. I can ride so well and pump
my tires up so far that we'd manage, but I don't fancy it. What are
you to me? I've been riding over the sea for months now, and all of
a sudden you want to join me for the last week? What would be the
point of that? The whole idea is for me to set a solo record. I can't
explain to all the people at the finish that you only joined me right
at the end. And I'd have to do my very best to keep the moped going
with two men riding on it. And what's more I've never practised
with a second man. How do I know what sudden movements you
might not make? It's all a question of dancing lightly over the water
on the moped, as they say,' the man continued, 'do you know
anything about tightrope walking?' Isaac, who didn't wholly understand the question, said he didn't. 'Well,' the man replied, 'you have
to keep your balance on the moped all the time and you have to
keep your tyres as high up against the waves as possible.' Then the
man said goodbye and climbed back down the ladder with his
moped. Isaac wanted to adjust the rope ladder a little, but the man
called out again, and this time over and over very loudly: 'Careful,
careful!' When the man got close to the water, he turned the engine
on full so that the wheels were spinning around in the air above the
water. Now and then the man touched the tyres to the surface of the
water very carefully, and at a given moment he sprang from the
rope ladder onto the raging moped with a sudden movement, and it
sped away at breakneck speed. It was starting to get a little lighter.
Isaac felt a touch dejected. Within a quarter of an hour the moped
had vanished over the horizon. Isaac went to bed for just an hour.
The next day, he confided to the radio operator what he'd witnessed
the night before. He shrugged his shoulders, and when Isaac perse-
vered, he started to laugh. An hour later the whole ship knew that

Isaac had seen a man riding over the water by night. Everyone laughed. When the day had ended, Isaac was very sleepy. But before going to bed he took a little stroll along to the poop deck. The sun had just gone down. It promised to be another fine night. It was a little cloudier now. Unconsciously, Isaac started scanning the water. But, naturally, the man on the moped was nowhere to be seen. Isaac felt more like crying than laughing; he didn't belong ashore, he didn't belong with the crew, he didn't even belong with the man on the moped. He looked at the dangerous, foaming propeller wash and the birds flying behind the ship. He felt himself to be a lonely man and he slowly came to the realisation that this was how things would always be. He lit up a cigarette and began humming a psalm, but he could scarcely hear his own voice. The wind had picked up and the propeller rose in and out of the water, and spun around in the air like a lunatic, then it fell back into the water with a heavy crash. Isaac looked at one of the sea birds and wished he could fly like that creature and land wherever he wanted. He wished he could fly behind the ships or far away over the horizon. Without realising it he began imitating the movements of the albatross' wings in the air. Quite by chance, the bosun saw him. He sniggered, because he could see that Isaac was standing there with his feet firmly rooted to the deck...

Envy

Margriet de Moor

translated by Paul Vincent

We still occasionally talk about Willy and Nora. Willy was our mother, and Nora our stepmother. Of course they never met.

How beautiful was Willy? Gorgeous! Tall, blonde, with those blue-veined hands, the kind that can gesture so expressively in a conversation, but busied themselves just as charmingly with riding boots and shoe polish, for example.

And cheerful too. Whenever we lay there bleating our hearts out, she had only to come in, in her white blouse, and had only to say 'My dear little lion-cubs, what are you lying about here for, come along with me...' for us to realise that there was a festive air in the house and the sun was flooding in through windows as high as the sky.

Willy Meeuwenoord was her name. Married at twenty two to a scion of an ancient Walloon family that had settled in Noordwijk. She had no problem with the fact that Gustave, our father, had burdened their union with two young sons from a previous marriage. Not a bit of it, she took the fat boys, who couldn't keep up at school, to her heart and the following summer gave birth to twins, girls, us. And six years later she fell off her horse after suffering an acute pain in her chest.

Willy and Nora. Whenever we think of them, we see them walking side by side under the poplars at the back of the house. Willy, in a close-fitting beige outfit, is drawing on a cigarette with a carefree expression, Nora, harassed-looking, stares straight ahead. Willy looks pale. Nora has bright red cheeks. Willy is thinking about horses, ocean-going ships, babies, summer nights, all at once. And in a minute a glass of wine. Nora is suffering in the heat. Ice tea with lemon would be wonderful. Willy was a darling who with her sea fisherman's gaze made sure her husband, fifteen years older, stopped dreaming since real life was a whole lot nicer. How did we know all that? We knew through Nadine, our step-sister. And all the softness vanished from Nora's brown eyes.

The evening they arrived! Our whole house crammed with suitcases and people trotting up and down the stairs! And we who had been told we were getting another mother, and a big sister into the bargain... '*Ah, mes petites pouces*, you need warmth!' said papa. We looked in bewilderment at the elbows and hips of the females who were settling into the rooms of the second and third floor and seemed to be getting terribly excited about the depth of the wardrobes. And papa who remained a picture of calm and opened the garden doors (it was August), and in the draught of air through the stairwell stopped one of those oh so restless women in her tracks and put his hands on her hips from behind.

That was our first chance to study Nora's face.

Of course she was pretty.

At nine o'clock we were all sitting in the drawing room. The strange things had been cleared away, and yet the furniture and the fire-irons in the form of three-masters seemed different from usual and our brothers were peering at the door with the expression of deaf-mutes. They were wearing their American sports shirts with wide short sleeves. After a silence Nadine got up. We hadn't paid any attention up to then, but we found that our step-sister's voice was as slow and full of sighs as the bass of a church organ.

'Why don't I go and make some coffee?'

She disappeared to the kitchen, came back and looked questioningly at us. Her voice was nothing like a church organ now, but very like the shock of a searchlight beam.

'Where did she keep the coffee creamer?'

That was her question. Willy. Where did Willy keep the coffee creamer? We smiled without looking at each other, and especially without looking at Nora in whom the awful affliction must have taken hold at that very moment. So the house remained as it had always been. With Willy as mistress of the chairs and tables, the dune landscapes, fire-irons, photos, clocks and tea services and the wind that you always felt when you walked barefoot down the hall. Our brothers mumbled 'so long' and got up to go dancing in Duna Deli as usual.

What a strange evening for a couple of tots. 'Take us to bed,' we said to Gustave. On the stairs our heads nodded on his shoulder, but our thoughts were creatures that never relaxed completely. Nadine needs a mouse, we felt, and that mouse is her mother. We know that Nadine can already feel the soft mouse wriggling in her jaws.

Night. The upper floors of a house on the edge of the dunes. The boys aren't back yet. The girls are asleep and so is Nadine, alone in the attic. In the balcony room Gustave puts his arm round his wife and tries to blow in her ear. But she twists her head away.

'*Je t'aime*, Nora.'

At the beginning we did not notice that much about her. When she appeared in the kitchen in the mornings last of all, thick mouth, heavy eyelids, she would sit down at table and wait until Nadine poured her a cup of coffee. 'I didn't sleep well,' was all she said. Or at most, 'I had a pain in my tummy.' Yet we knew that Nadine's words must have started affecting her deeply. Because the habit that Nadine acquired was polishing and waxing the rooms, finding something special every ten steps and then telling her mother about it while motioning with her hand. Sometimes it was the entire contents of the basement cupboard, sometimes one of Willy's old raincoats that she selected in order to introduce that peripatetic queen, Mummy, to Nora.

'Those are sink brushes,' she would explain, for example. 'She bought them at the door. Very well made, don't you think? They're mahogany.'

'Yes yes,' Nora would mumble, and we couldn't figure why she did not walk straight on but always stopped and listened, curious and troubled.

'… because when she fastened this coat, with wellingtons underneath and for good measure an old hat on her head, she looked like a tramp. She knew the coast not as a holiday-maker, but like a beach fisherman setting off after a stormy night with a bucket and a dragnet.'

What was Nadine talking about? Was she getting information from Gustave or was she just putting herself in Willy's shoes, guessing and distorting with all her senses. What we know for sure is that we lost Willy, as we had once known her, almost completely, so dissolved did she become in our stepsister's words.

'And on mornings like that she often…'

And what we know for sure is that Nora soon began stumbling on the stairs and knocking over flower vases, and that when we saw her sitting at her dressing table mirror through the half-open door, with her ramrod-straight neck, we were looking at a woman who could now look not just at her appearance but at the whole world from only one point of view: Willy was more beautiful than Nora.

That happened in those first few weeks, when she still went into every room in the house and into the village to shop, with us following her like puppies and carrying everything. It was the summer holidays, and flags were waving everywhere. Later, as Nadine's stories expanded, she no longer went out. As soon as Gustave had driven off in his car, her smile turned into the vacant expression of someone who has lost everything. She went back upstairs where she often sat for hours in a leather chair in a little room full of books.

'What's the matter with her?' we once asked Nadine.

'Nothing. Just take her some tea.'

The more languid the mother became, the faster the daughter dashed about. There were days when Nadine not only cooked and did the washing, but also dragged the carpets outside and shifted the wardrobes about so violently that we would have to be soft in the head not to realise that *this* was the house our step-sister wanted to work in for the rest of her life. Finally she would invite her mother downstairs to have a breather and talk a bit in a house smelling of beeswax.

They sat on the sofa. We lay in the conservatory. Next to the sofa was a vase full of fluffy feathers. On the table a soda fountain. Below the veranda, directly behind the open doors was a flowing gardenia. We looked from the flowers to Nora's face. From the bright red to the glowing pink. Nadine was telling her that the whole house had been done up about eight years ago and that to mark the occasion a party was given here that they still talk about in the village. Everyone had been dressed, she said, in a costume connected with the sea, and Willy had hit on the idea of having her trousers, blouse and sash copied from an eighteenth-century painting.

'You've seen it hanging, of course, here in the stairwell. "Macedonian pirate".'

The way Nadine told a story was out of the ordinary. There was a cadence in her voice, as if she did not need to think about anything because she was speaking words that somehow already existed, she sighed less and if we had closed our eyes we could have sworn she was reading aloud to us from a lovely thick book on her lap. She told us that Willy had made a big impression. That every-one loved her. We fidgeted and started picking our noses with blank looks on our faces, now Willy, Mummy, was wandering around in a story that everyone knew and for all we knew had been written down by someone.

That she danced all night.

Then we met Nora's eyes. And there was such dark detestation in her look that Nadine then started talking about Willy's beautiful blonde hair that she often wore in a braid on her back and how Gustave loved combing out that hair that he thought smelled of sun and wind, so that we realised what telling a story meant.

Nora. Dark patches where her eyes were. Cheeks burning red.

Telling a story is turning round one fact after another until they suddenly click into place and fit perfectly together: Gustave loved Willy more than Nora.

He put his arms round her. He said darling. He kissed her when he came home. One afternoon when he came back unexpectedly, he could not understand why on earth she was sitting there among the books, in that chair, and pulled her to her feet by her hands. Through the tall coloured-glass doors we saw him walking into the garden with her. It was still summer and oppressively warm. Just past the gardenia he started on about, darling and love again... He also talked about lovely, round, soft, and slid his hand inside her neckline, he said, 'Listen, Nora, from the day I met you...' He rubbed his cheek across her head, and started kissing her again.

But he could not convince her of the one thing that mattered. And when he broke a branch of the creeper and stuck the red flower behind her ear, she must have thought: I can't stand it any longer.

I can't stand her garden and her creeper any longer, her terrace with the glazed pots and the steps that lead up to her house with its two storeys, I can't stand her drawing room any longer, her kitchen, her stairs that take you up in a curve to the first landing with four rooms behind four doors, her bed, her bedspread with the faded tassels, her mirrored wardrobe where you still saw her green eyes and white skin shining, her bathroom and God knows why her turtledoves on the wide window-sill, that you see from the bath sitting cooing with their eyes closed: I can stand those least of all.

And one day she fell ill and stayed in bed.

Her pins. Her paper clips. Her elastic bands.

That afternoon we were sitting lazily and sadly among our toys on the floor. On the other side of the hall was the room with the curtains drawn where Nora had been lying for a week complaining about the heat; consequently all the doors and windows had to be opened against each other. We heard our step-sister walking about and sometimes we saw her too, with plates and drink glasses on a tray which if you knew no better would remind you of someone preparing a birthday party. In reality it was only a few days before Nora left our house for good and as if we already knew we kicked sulkily at the bottom of our bed and leafed through a book resting against one of the legs with a heavy feeling behind our eyes.

At a certain moment Nadine was back, on the other side of the hall. Invisible to us, she shifted a few objects around, we heard tinkling and imagined she was pouring water. The bed creaked.

'Is that you again?'

'Yes, it's me, Nadine.'

We heard a flopping sound and pictured Nadine plumping up the pillows.

'What are you doing?'

'I've come to sit with you for a bit.'

Then we heard the voice again, slow and soft like sighing in church.

'I think it was a Monday,' said Nadine. 'On Monday 15th March she got the idea in her head of riding along the beach from Noordwijk to Wassenaar.'

A jolt went through us. In our alarm we sat up on our knees. Her horse, we heard, was in her brother's stables, Meeuwenoord, right behind the dunes next to the Palace hotel. At the fish stall she left the sandy path and turned left onto the beach, with its familiar view of shacks, driftwood and incidental walkers. She felt good. February had been joyless because of a bout of flu that had dragged on for weeks, and had shut her off from the snow-white winter on the other side of the windows. Today the spring sun was shining. The air felt fresh and damp. She dug her heels into the flanks of the horse and refused to pay attention to the unpleasant tightness that had remained in her chest since her illness.

At Katwijk she had to go slightly inland because of the estuary. She reached the sluices, crossed and on the other side hurried down, leaping on her horse as if some appointment further on were making her impatient. After the cobbles of the promenade, fifteen kilometres of soft ground stretched ahead of her. She bent forward, elbows loose. Breathing heavily with joy she heard, as if through a pipe, the dull roar of the sea and saw a flock of birds take off from the sand and skim away just above her head. Before she realised she had charged past post eighteen, post twenty-three and a board that said DANGER NO ENTRY.

Nadine's voice fell silent. Suddenly we realised that we were sobbing. And when the silence continued, we heard that someone across the hall was sobbing with us. It couldn't be Nadine, we knew, because she now appeared in the doorway with her arms full of towels and went towards the stairs, on her way, we knew, to the washroom in the scullery.

And Nora cried aloud. Not with emotion, we knew, and not from grief at Willy Meeuwenoord speeding along there towards her assignation with fate, unforgettably beautiful in her jacket and jodhpurs and trailing her loosened hair in gleaming strands behind her.

Author Notes

Anna Blaman (1905-1960) was considered one of the most important authors of her generation following the publication of her novel *Lonely Adventure*. In her work she depicted the problems of modern life openheartedly, without illusion, without hypocrisy. Nevertheless, her work was often regarded as negative or offensive because of her frank homo-eroticism. Recognition of her work was eventually confirmed by the award of the PC Hooft Prize in 1957.

Bernlef (1937) is one of the Netherlands foremost contemporary authors. He has published many collections of poetry, short stories, novels and essays. He is best known for his novels *Out of Mind* and *Public Secret*. He has won many prizes including the PC Hooft Prize, the Constanijn Huygens Prize and the AKO Literature Prize. He has also published two novels in English with Faber & Faber, translated by Paul Vincent.

JMA Biesheuvel (1939) is an extremely colourful writer who rarely obeys the laws of the genre that he exercises. This results in wonderful narratives that alternate between heartrending realism and the almost magical. The faith of his parents and his struggle with it plays a central role in his work. Until he was institutionalised at the age of 26 he wanted to become a minister. His sojourn at the asylum proved to be a rich source of inspiration. In the 1970s and 1980s he published many collections of short stories, for which he was awarded the Alice van Hahuys Prize and the F Bordewijk Prize.

Hugo Claus (Belgium, 1929) is a poet, novelist and playwright and perhaps the most important living author in the Dutch-language area. He moved to Paris in 1947, where he met Antonin Artaud. He also came into contact there with the experimentalist Dutch writers of the 1950s. His first novel was published in 1950, his first collection of poems in 1954. His masterpiece *The Sorrow of Belgium* appeared in 1983. He has won more prizes than any other Dutch-language writer and has been nominated for the Nobel Prize.

Cola Debrot (1902-1981) is often called the founder of Dutch-Antillean literature. He was a trailblazer for Antillean writers with such works as *My Sister the Negress* (1935), *Confession in Toledo* (1945) and *Prayer for Camille Willocq* (1949). Debrot emphasised the independent nature of the Antillean and convinced his countrymen that Caribbean culture is 'mixed'. Later in life he became the United Nations representative for the Dutch Antilles and from 1962 to 1970 served as the Governor of the islands.

Margriet de Moor (1941) is one of the Netherlands best-selling authors. She grew up in a large Catholic family of ten children. In 1984 she founded a successful artists salon with her husband, the sculptor Heppe de Moor. She made her debut with the short story collection *Seen on the Back* in 1998. Four years later she won the AKO Literature Prize for her novel *First Grey Then White Then Blue*.

Harry Mulisch (1927) is the author of a number of internationally best-selling novels, including *The Procedure*, *The Assault* (which was made into the film that won the 1987 Oscar for Best Foreign Film), and *The Discovery of Heaven* (recently made into a film starring Stephen Fry). He has also published short stories, essays, poetry, plays and philosophical works.

Gerard Reve (1923) published his remarkable debut short story *The Decline of the Family Boslowits* in 1946. This was followed by the classic novel *The Evenings* in 1947. In 1953 Reve published his first book in English *The Acrobat and Other Stories*. From the mid 1960s on Reve came out openly about his homosexuality. He caused a minor scandal when accepting the PC Hooft Prize in 1969 by kissing Minister Klompé on the cheek. Five years later he was knighted. Once the genie was out of the bottle as regards explicit sex passages Reve found the themes that he would use throughout the rest of his work – drinking, forcing young boys into sexual slavery, Mary's mercy, the consolation of the Catholic faith and the insincerity of Communism.

J Slauerhoff (1898-1936) was the exemplary *poète maudit*. He travelled to Asia, Africa and South America as a ship's doctor and died at the age of 38 after acquiring an incurable disease in the tropics. Of the pre-war modernists, he has remained the most popular because his poetry, novels and short stories combine the romantic concerns of the nineteenth century with the contemporary idiom of Modernism.

Willem van Toorn (1935) is one of the Netherlands' most respected contemporary poets, novelists and short story writers. He is also the editor of the leading literary magazine *Raster*. His work is characterised by subtle understatement and brilliant descriptive power. Recent publications include a *Collected Poems* and the novels *The River and Steam*. He has translated such figures as Pavese and Kafka. His poetry has been published in English in the TLS and by Seren, translated by Craig Raine.